OCEAN CITY SUNGLOW

CLAUDIA VANCE

CHAPTER ONE

"Hey. I was just thinking about you. I'm guessing you made it to Vermont safely?" Matt asked after he answered Lauren's call.

Lauren nodded as she rolled down the windows to air the truck out. "I did. The flight went smoothly, and I was able to pick up the moving truck rental right from the airport. It stinks horribly, though. It smells like the people who had it last hid dead fish throughout it. Actually, you know what? I need to get out … now," she said, hopping out of the truck with her phone.

"I'd go back inside and ask for a new one," Matt said, thoroughly grossed out for her.

Lauren nodded as she peered back into the truck, spotting some items underneath the driver's seat. "I think I found the culprit. There's a bunch of trash under my seat. Appears to be old rotten food. I'm going to go let them know now."

Matt shook his head. "Good. Don't they have people who check for all that before they rent it out? I don't get it."

"Me neither. Let me call you back after I get this sorted out," Lauren said as she walked back inside and right up to a worker at the front desk.

Ten minutes later, she was back in the truck, dialing Matt again. "Well, it wasn't the outcome I wanted, but it'll do," she said after he answered.

"What did they say?" Matt asked.

Lauren started the engine. "It's the only rental truck they have left today. They cleaned up the mess, but the smell still lingers. They gave me a discount. I guess it will work."

Matt rolled his eyes. "That's the worst. I'm sorry. I hope you can get the smell out before your long drive back to Ocean City."

"Me too," Lauren said as she put her phone on speaker and pulled the truck out of the parking lot.

Matt paused for a moment. "I know everything is so new between us, but it wouldn't have been an inconvenience for me to have come with you to help out. Packing up a truck and driving six-plus hours back sounds like a lot to take on solo."

Lauren blushed. "I know, but you're understaffed at Jungle Surf. Most of your employees are back in college already. I didn't want you to have to scramble to find help."

Matt ran his hand through his hair as he walked out of Jungle Surf and onto the sunny Ocean City Boardwalk. "It wouldn't have been a problem, but it is crowded for mid-September. The kids are back in school, and it's still hot out. You should see how many people are out here. What's the temperature in Vermont?"

"I think it's around seventy degrees today," she said as she took the exit for the highway.

Matt nodded. "It's about eight-five here. Lots of people sunbathing on the beach. Plenty of people in the shop too. I can't complain about staying open later this year."

"How late are you staying open?" Lauren asked.

"Probably mid-October. In the past years, I've always closed the weekend after Labor Day. We're going to see how it goes this year, but I talked to some other store owners, and they said they were busy right into October."

"Do you have enough workers to get through until then?"

Matt shrugged. "I hope so, or it may just be me and my family filling in here or there," he said with a little laugh. "This year might end up being a big learning experience, but I'm ready."

Lauren smiled. "This year has been nothing but a learning experience for me. I'm still deciding on how or if I should keep Chipper's open in the offseason. For now, I'm glad I decided to close up to give my staff a two-week break after that busy summer season. My family always kept Chipper's seasonal and closed in the offseason, but there are breakfast places that stay open year-round and do well."

Matt nodded as he walked across the boardwalk back into Jungle Surf. He eyed a succulent for sale and pulled off some dead leaves. "Well, you've got a lot of options. If you decide to close in September or October, you could pursue other ventures in the offseason, or you could give it a shot and stay open all year to see how it goes."

"You're right. I guess I have a couple weeks to really think about it. I just don't know what other ventures I could pursue at this time or if it would be too much to take on right now. I just closed on my new house and acquired my family's business in a matter of months," Lauren said as she moved the truck into the right lane. "How are sales at the store today?"

Matt walked behind the register and opened it up, then cracked open a roll of quarters to dump them in. "Let's see," he said as he closed the register. He then pulled out the notebook he kept under the counter and flipped through the pages, landing on the last one with writing. "Only about a hundred dollars in sales so far. Not good, but it is early. In the summer months, it would be much more than that by now. It does make me a little nervous about staying open until October, but I have to try, or I'll never know if it's worth it. I'm betting the places that serve food and drinks are still making a killing, though. You should see the lines they have."

Lauren paused in thought. "You should ask the other apparel and gift shops how they do in the offseason. It could very well be different than the places that serve food and drinks. Oh, here's my exit," she said as she got off the highway and drove towards a cute suburban town.

"Where are you headed first?" Matt asked as he shut the notebook and walked from behind the counter towards the clothing racks.

"Veronica and Dan's—good friends of mine since college. They're going to help me pack the truck, then I'm spending the night at their place. It's the one part of this trip I'm looking forward to."

Matt smiled as he adjusted a couple of surf brand T-shirts on the rack. "Oh, that's good. I guess you're not looking forward to packing the truck and driving it all the way back here?"

Lauren shook her head. "No. In fact, I'd thought about not coming back to Vermont at all and just selling the stuff I'd left in storage instead. I'm not comfortable driving this truck. It's weird only using my side mirrors to see, and even though it's a smaller size truck, it's still so big and bulky. Honestly, it's scary."

"Just drive carefully. Make sure you have your GPS set up and plan out where the rest stops are in case you need to use the bathroom. Find some good audiobooks and podcasts, pack some snacks and drinks, and you'll be set," Matt said as some customers walked past him towards the register to check out.

"It sounds like you've done this before," Lauren said with a chuckle as she pulled up to a cute green Cape Cod with vibrant green grass.

"I have. I don't mind a long drive if I've got a great audiobook or friend to talk with the whole time," Matt said as he walked towards the customers by the counter.

"Well, I just pulled up to my friends' house. Thanks for the chat. I'll give you a call later to let you know how it's going."

"Perfect. Talk to you soon," Matt said with a bit of pep in his heart.

* * *

Lauren hopped out of the truck and headed towards the Cape Cod's front door, noticing there was only one car in the driveway. She knocked a few times, but nobody answered.

"That's weird," she said aloud as she called Veronica's number.

Veronica picked up immediately. "Hey, girl. That was quick. Are you boarding your flight?"

Lauren laughed and looked at her watch, noticing it was 10 a.m. on the dot. "Not only did I board, I've flown all the way to Vermont and am already at your front door."

Veronica widened her eyes. "What? You're at my door?"

Lauren looked at the number on the house to make sure she wasn't going crazy. "Yep. I'm here."

Veronica slapped her forehead. "I had written down that you'd be arriving around noon. Dan and I stepped out to run an errand about a half hour away for his mom. She's laid up after knee replacement surgery. I don't even have a hidden spare key to direct you to. I'm so sorry."

Lauren waved her hand in the air. "It's totally fine. You know what? I'll just go pick up some coffee and breakfast …. Maybe read a little of my book. Take your time."

Veronica shook her head, feeling frustrated with herself. "I'm so sorry. We should be home in an hour or so. I'll call you when we head back. If you want to hang out on the back patio, feel free. I can't wait to see you, though. We have so much to catch up on."

"We certainly do," Lauren said as she headed back to the truck and shut the door. "I'll see you soon," she said, then they both hung up. She buckled up, put the truck into drive, then headed towards her favorite coffee shop in the area.

Lauren stopped at a stop sign and paused in thought. She was only a short distance from her house, the one they just sold in the divorce. That house was so special to her. Should she drive by and see it? Would it break her heart even more? She nodded, put her blinker on, and turned right.

Five minutes later, she was driving slowly through her old neighborhood. She stopped the truck in the street as a cat ran by in front of her and rolled down her windows. "Jasper!" Lauren yelled out. "You're still finding a way to sneak outside, I see. You better get home, mister," she said while pointing to his home.

She watched as Jasper moseyed back to his front porch and sat on a cushioned chair, then she kept driving slowly until she got to her old house. She hadn't realized she'd stopped the truck in the middle of the street until she caught herself staring at her beloved former home. The hedges and flower beds looked beautiful and well maintained. The front door had been painted a light beige color, and there were long sheer white curtains in the windows in place of the blinds that Lauren had put up. A basset hound popped up in the front window and peered out. Catching a glimpse of the moving truck, he let out a howl.

These new owners are going to think I'm a creep staring like this, Lauren thought to herself when a knock on the passenger window startled her. She looked over to see her old neighbor, Sue, smiling ear to ear while holding a coffee mug.

"I knew it. I told Chad that the woman sitting in the moving truck looked like you, and I was right! What are you doing here?" Sue asked excitedly.

Lauren held her chest and laughed, her heart still racing from the unexpected knock on the window. "Sue, it is so good to see you. I'm actually back in town to pick up my stuff from the storage unit. I bought a house in Ocean City, New Jersey, believe it or not."

Sue's mouth dropped open. "You did? I thought for sure you'd be back after the summer. Why don't you come in for some coffee? Are you hungry?"

Lauren nodded. "I was about to go get some coffee and breakfast. I'd love some."

Sue pointed to the open parking spot in front of her house. "Park the truck there and come inside. I can make you a breakfast sandwich, and Chad has this wonderful fresh-roasted coffee from Mexico. You've got to try it."

Lauren smiled and parked the truck then followed Sue into her cozy house, but not before catching the eyes of Jasper next door.

"I see Jasper is still escaping the house," Lauren said as she walked behind Sue into the kitchen.

Sue rolled her eyes. "Lilly and Stu have tried everything. He had been an outdoor cat when they rescued him, and that's part of the problem."

Lauren sat at the kitchen table as Chad walked in. "Lauren! It is you. Guess you were right, hon," Chad said as he gave Sue a kiss on the cheek.

Sue smirked. "I told you. This twenty-twenty vision does not lie."

Chad rolled his eyes. "She was being nosy, per usual. Had to see who was sitting in that moving truck outside."

Sue gave him a look, then poured some of the hot coffee into a mug and handed it to Lauren. "Help yourself to the creamers in the fridge and sugar on the table."

"OK, I'm heading to the VFW. I'll have Sue fill me in on everything when I get home. It was good seeing you, Lauren," Chad said as he put his ball cap on and walked towards the front door.

Lauren smiled as she added some sugar to her coffee. "Good seeing you too."

Sue watched as Chad left the house, then proceeded to add

butter and a couple of eggs to a sizzling hot pan. "So, how are you? Tell me everything. I haven't seen you in months. I miss having you as a neighbor. My gosh, and the way it all ended. I hate that I was the one to tell you …"

Lauren shook her head as she got up to grab some oat milk (a staple Sue always had) out of the fridge, then poured it into her coffee. "Sue, I'm glad you told me. I don't think anyone else would have, honestly."

Sue shrugged. "I still feel like I ruined a marriage."

Lauren sighed as she sat back down, stirred her coffee, then took a sip. It was fantastic, just like Sue had said. "You didn't ruin a marriage. Steven did. Remember that. Plus, things are going pretty well in Ocean City. My parents are there. I'm taking over the family restaurant. I've got a new house in a prime location for a bargain price. There's also someone new …"

"Someone new?" Sue asked as she popped two slices of sourdough bread into the toaster.

Lauren smiled as she felt her face flush. "His name is Matt. It's really new though. I'm trying not to fall too head over heels too quick."

"Oh, am I loving this for you. Do you miss Vermont?"

Lauren nodded. "I do. I miss my house. It's so weird to see other people living in it. I feel like I'm in an alternate reality, being on this street and my house not being my house anymore. It does seem well cared for, and that makes me happy, I guess."

Sue buttered the toasted bread, added the eggs, cheese, and sliced tomato, then cut it corner to corner before putting it on a plate and handing it to Lauren. "Well, I've seen Steven drive by the house many times since you guys sold it. I just wasn't expecting to see you do it."

Lauren took a bite of the delicious egg-and-cheese sandwich. "I haven't spoken to him in months. I have no idea where he moved to. It was like a closed chapter. No looking back. I'm guessing he misses our old house, too, though. It was special. It's just crazy how your life can change so drastically within a year," Lauren said as she felt her stomach turn at the thought of Steven.

CHAPTER TWO

Both Veronica's and Dan's eyes widened as Lauren opened the rolling door to the storage unit. "This is all yours?" Veronica asked as she moved closer to get a better look.

Lauren shrugged sheepishly. "Yes. All these pieces are family heirlooms or vintage pieces I fell in love with at Habitat ReStore. Does it seem a bit much?"

Dan laughed. "It might take us an extra hour to pack it in the truck, but we'll fit it all in somehow."

Lauren covered her mouth. "Should I have gotten a larger moving truck? Jeez, I didn't even think of that."

Veronica sized up the truck. "We'll figure it out, I'm sure. Right, Dan?" she said while leaning on his shoulder.

Dan rolled up his sleeves. "Right. Now, let's start moving stuff. I'll coordinate where everything goes in the truck."

Lauren breathed a sigh of relief. "What would I have done without you two? I can't thank you enough," she said while picking up the end of a desk that Dan already had the other end of.

Two hours later, the truck was packed to the ceiling with not even a foot to spare, and Lauren had managed to pull the door down and lock it with a padlock.

"We'll meet you at the house," Veronica said while blotting the sweat on her chest and arms with a paper towel.

Dan stood by the car. "Yeah, let's get showers and go out to dinner. We need someone else to cook for us after all that heavy lifting."

"Definitely," Lauren said as she got into the driver's seat of the truck. "I'll see you guys over there."

* * *

By 5 p.m., they were laughing together with glasses of wine—and the most beautiful bread basket—at a small table lit by candles in Vincenzo's.

Veronica took a sip of her wine, then burst out laughing again. "We probably should have eaten the bread before we ordered drinks, and why did they seat us at the most romantic table in the entire place?"

Dan pointed to the rest of the restaurant, which had mainly booths and tables with brighter recessed lighting above them. "Right? It feels like we're in a totally different restaurant over here."

Lauren laughed then took a sip of her chardonnay. "Who knows, but I can't see a thing on this menu," she said as she turned on the flashlight on her phone.

"Shine some this way," Veronica said as she inched closer to Lauren with her menu.

The server suddenly appeared. "Are you all ready to order, or do you need more time?"

"I'm ready," Lauren said while looking at Veronica and Dan.

"OK, you go ahead first," Dan said while staring at the menu.

"Great. I'll have the lasagna, please," Lauren said.

"I'll have the chicken marsala," Veronica said.

"And I'll have the mussels and spaghetti," Dan said as he gathered the menus and handed them to the server.

The server wrote everything down in her book, then walked away.

Veronica stared ahead towards the front door as a couple walked in. "Oh no."

Dan followed her gaze and stared with her, scratching his beard, then glanced at Lauren, who was too busy checking her phone to notice anything.

Veronica looked at Dan, tapped him with her foot, and shook her head. "No."

Lauren looked up from her phone with a smile, then pulled a piece of the warm crusty bread out of the basket and took a bite. "So, tell me, what's new with you two? I feel like we barely got to talk too in-depth today with all the work we were doing."

Veronica glanced at Dan. "Well, I got promoted at the firm, and Dan has taken over his dad's construction business. This all happened quite recently."

"Wow. That's awesome. I'm so happy for you guys," she said holding her wineglass out.

They clinked glasses, then Veronica discreetly glanced towards the couple at the front of the restaurant and back at Lauren. "But what about you? Tell us everything."

Lauren smiled. "Well, as you know, I settled on the house in Ocean City. I can't believe it. Then, there's Chipper's. I'm now running it, but I have so many decisions to make in the offseason. Ocean City does most of its business seasonally even though there's plenty of people that live there year-round. Then, there's Matt …"

Veronica made eyes at Dan then set her glass down. "Did I hear *Matt*? As in a man?"

Lauren laughed. "Yes. A man. He's my neighbor."

"OK, tell me more," Veronica said as her eyes widened.

Lauren took a deep breath and felt her heart flutter a little as she started thinking about him. "He owns a neat surf shop on the Ocean City Boardwalk. He played pro baseball for a bit, but an injury got in the way of that. He surfs. He drives a Jeep, and he really likes plants."

"What does he look like? Do you have a photo?" Veronica asked.

Dan shook his head and laughed. "This is turning into girl talk."

Veronica playfully smacked his arm. "Aren't you curious, too, hon? Our Lauren has found a love interest," she said as she looked towards the couple at the front of the restaurant again.

Lauren pulled out her phone and scrolled for a bit, then turned it towards Veronica and Dan. "This is him."

Dan grabbed the phone. "Jeez. He's ripped."

Veronica snatched the phone from his hands. "Let me see. Oh my. Wow ... that's all I'm going to say."

Dan rolled his eyes playfully. "I hope you say 'wow' about your man over here too."

Veronica kissed him on the cheek. "Of course."

Lauren took her phone back and stared at the photo of Matt leaning against his Jeep holding a surfboard. "Everything is very new, though. It's been such a whirlwind summer —" Lauren stopped her sentence as she looked across the restaurant, noticing a man standing up. "Is that ...?"

Veronica and Dan glanced in that direction. "It is. We saw him come in earlier, but we were hoping you wouldn't see him," Veronica said as she took a sip of her wine.

Lauren felt her stomach turn into knots as she stared with them from the dark corner. "Is he ... with someone?"

Veronica nodded. "He is."

Lauren's heart raced. "I wonder if it's ... her. The one he cheated on me with."

Dan cut in. "Lauren, don't even look that way. Don't let Steven hold any space in your head. You've moved on to bigger and better things."

Lauren nodded as her stomach grew sicker and sicker. "Oh, I know. I certainly have, but it's because I pushed all of this out of my mind, and now it's right in front of me to deal with, and he's with *her* most likely."

"Do you want to get our food to go?" Veronica asked. "We can eat takeout in the living room with a funny movie. It'll be fun!"

Lauren went into a daze. "I don't want to do that. Maybe we can just ignore them," she said as she looked over to see the woman with him standing up then walking to the bathroom. "It's her, the one he cheated on me with. Unreal."

"Excuse me! Could we get our meals to go?" Dan yelled out to a passing server. "We haven't seen our server in a while and have to get going."

"OK, I'll let them know," the server said, hurrying by.

Lauren took a deep breath. "I feel bad. I feel like our meal is ruined now."

Dan shook his head. "Look, it's too dark over here anyway, and these chairs are uncomfortable," he said trying to make her feel better. "We'll sneak out the back entrance, get home with our meals, get into pj's, and eat our food on the couch. It'll be like the old times when we would all hang out in college."

After they paid, they all stood up and gathered their things. Dan and Veronica walked towards the back door, but Lauren stopped and turned to the front of the restaurant one last time. Steven was sitting there alone, and they locked eyes for a few seconds before Lauren ducked out the door behind her friends.

* * *

"Wait. So you two have been married twenty years? For real?" Lauren asked while taking a bite of her to-go lasagna while sitting in her pajamas on the sectional couch.

"Yes. Can you believe it? It feels like we just got married,"

Veronica said as she cut a piece of her chicken marsala and popped it into her mouth.

Dan sat with his legs crisscrossed in the recliner as he dug into his spaghetti. "Best twenty years of my life, I must say."

Veronica held her heart and stared at Dan. "You are the sweetest. It really has been many great years with you. Wouldn't change it for the world."

"Aw. You guys," Lauren said, feeling sentimental about them.

Veronica glanced back at Lauren. "I know we didn't talk about it much, but you've been doing pretty good since the divorce?"

Lauren nodded. "Much better than I thought I'd be doing. It still hurts sometimes, though, because the life we built together for all those years just crumbled so fast. A lot of work went into that. A lot of the best years of my life were invested in that marriage."

Dan shook his head. "Well, he's a fool. A cheating fool. I'm glad we got out of that restaurant when we did."

Lauren cleared her throat. "I think he saw me."

Veronica sat up straight. "You do? How so?"

"As we were leaving, I quickly looked his way, and we locked eyes. Then, I was out the door seconds later. That was definitely one of the women he cheated on me with, though. I don't know why, but I think it bothered me more that it was her with him and not someone new, you know?"

Veronica glanced at Dan. "Oh, I totally get that. He essentially chose her over you."

Dan chimed in. "You know, I never really liked Steven. He was always so pretentious about a lot of things. He'd scoff if I drank a Bud Light and not some beer from a local microbrewery when we'd all hang out. He always talked over you during a conversation, and my gosh, what was up with that bouffant hairstyle and handlebar mustache he had recently? I mean, some people pull it off well, but he looked like he was playing a character."

Lauren chuckled. "I love how the truth comes out now. I felt the same way about that mustache. It definitely felt like he was trying to fit in with a crowd that he was not a part of, but I never told him that. I didn't want to hurt his feelings, but these women he cheated on me with seemed to be part of that hipster crowd he so badly wanted to be a part of. I guess he got what he wanted."

Veronica dropped her fork on her plate and pushed it away from her on the coffee table. "I'm happy for you. You've moved on. Now you're living this exciting life at the Jersey Shore."

Lauren laughed. "I don't know if *exciting* is the word I'd use, as I'm taking over our family restaurant and moving into a fixer-upper. We'll say work in progress."

Dan stood up and grabbed their empty plates. "Well, you ladies can hang out and chat while I clean up."

"Thanks, babe," Veronica said as she watched Dan make his way to the kitchen. She glanced back at Lauren. "So, I'm deciding if I should tell you this …."

"What?" Lauren asked as she pulled her knees into her chest.

"I know a bit more about Steven than I've let on this whole visit. I didn't feel it was appropriate to tell you, but I'm thinking I should."

Lauren widened her eyes. "What do you know?"

Veronica swallowed hard. "That woman he was with at the restaurant … the one he cheated on you with … that's my hairstylist."

Lauren covered her mouth with her hand. "OK, I was not expecting to hear that. Did you just figure that out tonight?"

Veronica shook her head. "No, I've known for a while now because I've been to the salon a lot the past year to get my roots done, and my stylist loves to yap about her life to me during the appointment."

"What has she said?" Lauren asked, starting to feel her heart race.

"She was going on and on about a new guy she was seeing named Steven. I, of course, never assumed it was your Steven because why would I? He was married to you. She was telling me about how they would go for romantic walks at Red Rocks Park—"

"That was our park. He proposed to me there. We went there all the time together. It was special to us, and here he was taking *her* there? When was she telling you all of this?" Lauren asked.

Veronica thought for a moment. "Last September maybe? But I had no idea it was Steven your husband, otherwise, I would have said something to you."

Lauren took a deep breath. "I feel like I'm going to be sick. So, he's been cheating for a lot longer than he said. He told me it had just started. Who knows how many years he'd been cheating on me. I feel like everything was one big lie."

"I shouldn't have told you. I'm so sorry," Veronica said as she reached over and touched Lauren's hand.

Lauren shook her head. "No, I'm glad you told me. I think it's pushing me to really make the life for myself that I deserve because that life with him wasn't it. What's her name, by the way?"

"Chrissy."

Lauren scratched her chin. "What's funny is Sue, my neighbor, had told me they saw him with multiple women at the house while I was away for work. Seems he may have been cheating on me *and* Chrissy. I wonder if Chrissy knew he was married."

"I don't think so. She spilled everything whenever I sat in her chair, and I specifically remember her saying that Steven had been separated from his wife and was in the process of a divorce."

Lauren rolled her eyes. "You think you know someone."

Just then, Dan appeared. "Hon, did you tell her yet?"

Lauren glanced at Veronica with widened eyes. "What now?"

Veronica laughed. "No, I haven't. Guess I should tell her now. I'm driving back to Ocean City with you."

Lauren cocked her head back in shock. "What? Why?"

"Because you shouldn't drive all that way alone in a big ol' truck, that's why. Plus, I need some adventure in my life. Anyway, Dan's coming too. He's going to fly down and meet us."

Dan nodded proudly. "When I heard you bought a fixer-upper on the bay, I knew I had to see what I could help out with."

Lauren smiled. "Guys, this is incredible news, but please don't take off all this time from work on my account. Don't you want to use that time to go relax on an island somewhere?"

Veronica laughed. "We already have that vacation planned for December. We both work jobs that give us freedom to take off days when we want. So, it's no problem at all. We're excited."

CHAPTER THREE

"Where are we?" Veronica asked as she glanced at the GPS.

Lauren squinted to see through the fog on the road ahead of them. "I think we've reached New York, but I'm not quite sure."

Veronica paused in thought. "That makes sense. We should be hitting New York by now. Let me know when you want me to take over the wheel."

Lauren glanced at Veronica and smirked. "You are not driving this moving truck."

"Why not?" Veronica asked, confused.

"Because I've seen all the cars you've banged up," Lauren said, laughing.

"That was in college—many years ago," Veronica said. "I've improved my driving since then."

Lauren took a deep breath. "We'll see. Maybe I'll let you."

Just then, the voice on the GPS alerted them to get off at the next exit. Lauren saw the signs and took the off-ramp, following the directions into a little town.

"What in the boondocks is this place?" Veronica asked while staring out the window at a field full of run-down carnival rides behind a locked gate.

"I'm not sure, but it's strange that the GPS took us off the highway to here, isn't it?" Lauren said as she slowly navigated the winding road they were on.

They approached a little town full of dilapidated houses and buildings with boarded-up windows. The street was empty except for one man smoking a cigarette while riding an electric scooter past them on the sidewalk.

"This is getting a little scary," Veronica said as she tried to sink down into her seat away from the window.

Lauren locked the doors and nodded in agreement as she kept driving the truck past the downtown section and now through what appeared to be an area full of rental cabins with Adirondack chairs lining the front of each of them. "I think we're through the worst of it."

Veronica sat up in her seat and looked out the window. "OK, this I can do. Seems to be a vacation area. Lots of little inns and campground communities. This seems nice."

Lauren pointed ahead at somebody on the side of the road. "Are they waving at us?"

Veronica's eyes widened as they got closer. "It's a man in a cowboy hat and chaps holding a vacancy sign for the motel."

Lauren started laughing. "The things you see when you take long drives. In what world would someone pull into a motel because a cowboy was holding a sign?" she said while driving past.

Veronica looked in her side mirror, noticing a car behind them pulling into the motel parking lot. "Well, it seemed to work for the folks behind us."

Just then, the voice on the GPS boomed, "Take your next right."

Lauren turned right, putting them on another back road. "I'm hoping it puts us on the highway again soon. I don't understand this detour."

Veronica felt her stomach growl. "I'm starving. If you see a McDonald's or anything, can you stop?"

Lauren nodded. "Definitely. I'm starving too."

Another half hour of driving on winding back roads somewhere in New York and not coming across a single place to get food, they finally found something.

Veronica pointed ahead. "Stop there."

Lauren glanced at the sign as they pulled into the parking lot. "Sally's Slop?"

Veronica hopped out of the truck. "It better be good slop, because I'm ready to feast."

There was not one window on the entire building, and when they walked in through the front door, it seemed everyone inside stopped what they were doing to turn and look at them.

"It smells like 90s potpourri and fried fish in here. Maybe we should keep driving till we find something else," Lauren muttered under her breath to Veronica.

Veronica shrugged. "Look at all the people here. It can't be *that* bad, right?"

"Table for two?" the host asked as she hiked up her pantyhose under her skirt.

"Um, yes," Lauren said hesitantly.

Veronica and Lauren followed the host past the bar and to a large room in the back with one wall air-conditioning unit working overtime. The tables had bright-orange tablecloths and silk flowers in a vase next to the salt and pepper.

"This is weird," Lauren said as they sat down and opened the menus.

Veronica nodded. "It is, but it's going to give us a better road trip story, no?"

Lauren laughed as she looked down at the menu. "I don't know what to get. What kind of slop are they known for?"

An older guy sitting with his wife next to them spoke up. "First time here for you two?"

"Yes. We're just passing through and couldn't find anywhere to stop to eat until now," Veronica said.

The guy glanced at his wife. "Well, a little tip from some locals. Get the fried chicken. It's what they're known for. Try the coleslaw and fries with it too. Come dinnertime, they'll have a two-hour wait for this chicken. You stopped at a good time."

"Really? Well, guess that's what I'm getting. Thank you, sir," Veronica said as she closed the menu and pushed it aside.

"Same. Thank you," Lauren said.

Twenty-five minutes later, they had their drinks and their fried chicken platters had just arrived.

Veronica poured some of the honey that came on the side of the chicken, then took a crunchy bite. "Wow. Absolutely incredible. You have to add the honey, Lauren."

Lauren added her honey, bit into the chicken, and swallowed. "The best I've ever had. It's wonderfully crunchy and seasoned well."

"See, I told you," the man at the table next to them said while smiling with his wife. "Good, right?"

"It's fantastic," Veronica said as she stopped eating to take a sip of her drink.

Thirty minutes later, they were back in the moving truck. Lauren turned the GPS on and looked at the directions. "Finally! It's putting us back on the highway."

Veronica clapped her hands. "Hooray!"

It was smooth sailing on the highway as they sang to eighties songs until Lauren suddenly turned the volume down. "I want to thank you again for doing this road trip with me, and for all the help you and Dan have given me. It's truly appreciated," Lauren said as she kept her eyes on the road.

Veronica shrugged. "We're happy to do it. You know you're one of our favorite people in the world, right? Dan had to console me when you moved away this summer. I was pretty bummed for like a week."

"You were? Oh no. I'm sorry. You should have come down.

You will love Ocean City, but to be there during its prime in the summer is something else. It's a fun place," Lauren said.

"Well, I did visit once when I was a kid, growing up in North Jersey and all. We usually went to the beaches up near us, though."

"That's right. I forgot you lived in North Jersey."

"It was only for five years of my childhood, but I loved those years. I made so many friends at my school, and we were close in distance to some of my cousins from my mom's side. I had the perfect number of friends and family around to not feel lonely as an only child. Then, my dad got a job in Vermont, and that's where we ended up staying. I love Vermont, but I've always longed for New Jersey. People always thought I was crazy," Veronica said as she stared out the window.

Lauren nodded. "Those who aren't from New Jersey don't understand the appeal, but when you live here, you know where to find all the beauty. Sometimes I like that it's a well-kept secret."

* * *

Four hours later, they crossed into New Jersey.

"Finally!" Lauren yelled as they made their way down the turnpike. "The end of this journey is in sight. We've got two more hours."

Veronica rolled down her window and let the warm breeze smack her face. "Hallelujah!"

Lauren glanced at Veronica and laughed. "I guess you'll be flying home instead of driving, huh?"

Veronica nodded confidently. "Absolutely."

Lauren turned up the radio to a Cyndi Lauper song, then she and Veronica sang together at the top of their lungs before Lauren had to slam on the brakes.

"What is going on up there?" she asked as she slowed the truck to a stop behind the cars in front of them.

Veronica craned her neck out of the window. "It looks like it's backed up for miles. I don't see an end in sight to this traffic."

Lauren threw her head back on the headrest. "Great. Just great."

Veronica pointed at the sky. "See how it's sunny here and black clouds ahead of us? I wonder if that has something to do with it."

Slowly, the standstill traffic started to move, but at a crawl.

"How are we feeling about listening to an audiobook for a bit? It might be a nice change from music, no?" Lauren asked.

"Sounds perfect. Here, let me plug in my phone. I have some new audiobooks downloaded," Veronica said as she scrolled through her phone. "OK, here we go," she said as she hit play.

"*Janie's Playground*. Written by Stella Tate," the older female narrator started.

"What is this one about?" Lauren asked.

Veronica shrugged. "I'm not sure. Someone online said it was good."

The narrator continued to chapter one. "It was a cold, gloomy night on the long road to the family cabin. Janie knew she shouldn't have been driving to the cabin at this late hour, but this was important. A dead body had been found on the property that morning, wrapped in a tarp and hidden in the woods behind the cabin. The neighbors had found it after their dogs had alerted them."

Lauren stared at the road, completely engrossed in the story while Veronica looked up at the dark clouds starting to take over the sky above them.

"It was only an hour until Janie would get to the cabin, but a part of her wished it would take longer. She was alone and arriving to a possible murder scene. Her husband wasn't answering his phone, which was unlike him, and for the entire ride, she had to talk herself out of turning the car around and getting the heck out of Dodge. Suddenly, a flash lit up the sky, and thunder boomed!"

Lauren and Veronica both screamed as the skies above them opened and rain came pouring down all around them.

Veronica held her chest while taking deep breaths and paused the audiobook. "That timing almost gave me a heart attack. How were we so in sync with this book?"

Lauren shook her head. "That was unbelievable."

"Let's put a hold on that story. I'm thinking we need something more upbeat right now. Something to get us in the mood to drive into Ocean City, where glam, glitz, and sunblock await."

Lauren laughed as her phone rang. She answered it on speaker to keep her hands on the wheel.

"Hey," Matt said.

Veronica widened her eyes and mouthed to Lauren, "Is that *him*?"

Lauren smiled and nodded. "Hey, Matt. You're on speaker. My friend Veronica is here in the truck with me. We're at a slow crawl on the turnpike somewhere in North Jersey in the pouring rain."

"Oh, wow. Well, hi, Veronica! Looking forward to meeting you in person when you get to sunny Ocean City," Matt said as he watered some of the plants in his surf shop.

"Same here. I've heard a lot about you," Veronica said as she flashed a smile to Lauren.

Lauren cut in quickly. "OK, enough about that. We should be there in two hours, but with this traffic, maybe two and a half or three. We have the moving truck packed full, and Veronica's husband, Dan, is flying into Atlantic City tonight."

"Perfect. Looking forward to it. I'll be next door and ready to lend a hand," Matt said.

Veronica leaned towards the phone on the console. "Listen, Matt. I have some questions for you. Have some time?"

Lauren looked at Veronica with a confused face.

"Yeah, sure. Ask away," Matt said with a little laugh.

Veronica cleared her throat. "OK, since you're dating my good friend, I need to know a little more about you …"

"Oh, no," Lauren said, half frightened of what Veronica was going to say.

"First. What intentions do you have with my friend?" Veronica asked with a straight face.

Lauren fumbled with the phone. "OK, question time is over."

Matt chimed in, "No. I like this. Let me answer."

Lauren took a deep breath and stared at Veronica.

"My intentions … let's see. Well, I'd like to get to know Lauren more. We've only known each other for a few months now."

Lauren cut in. "Exactly. We've practically just met. It's too soon for this line of questioning, Veronica," she said, glancing at her friend.

Veronica shrugged.

"But …" Matt said, then paused. "My long-term intentions involve a lot more than getting to know you, Lauren."

Veronica bit her lip and bounced around her seat, trying to hold in her scream. Meanwhile, Lauren's face turned a shade of bright red.

Just then, the audiobook popped on unexpectedly. "The rain pounded on the roof of Janie's car while the road became difficult to see."

"Matt? Can you hear me?" Lauren yelled as Veronica fumbled with her phone, trying to turn off the audiobook to no avail.

Matt yelled back, "Not really. I hear some woman talking about rain."

Lauren laughed. "We're having a technical difficulty. Let me call you back in a bit."

Matt sighed as he ran his fingers through his hair. "Sounds good. Call when you get in. Stay safe."

The audiobook kept playing. "Janie pulled the car over on the dark road until the rain let up. She couldn't see a thing … except her childhood playground sitting directly to her right. The one she and her siblings would walk to whenever they visited the family cabin. This wasn't any old playground, though—"

"There!" Veronica finally got the audiobook turned off, and the truck became quiet. "I was impressed with his answer. He passed the test for sure," Veronica said.

Lauren playfully nudged her friend. "Your little test mortified me. Why would you put him on the spot like that? The poor guy didn't know how to answer, and he really shouldn't have to this early on."

Veronica side-eyed Lauren. "Oh, he knew how to answer. He likes you. A lot. I can tell. That's all I needed to hear."

"Really? That's it? You don't have any other questions?" Lauren asked.

Veronica thought for a moment. "Well, there are some others. Just be glad I didn't get to those."

Lauren scratched her chin. "Well, now I need to know the other questions."

"I'll tell you one. I was going to ask him if he says *pork roll* or *Taylor ham*. I feel it's important," Veronica said, trying to hold a serious expression.

Lauren burst out laughing.

CHAPTER FOUR

"So, this is it—9th Street Bridge to Ocean City," Lauren said, feeling relief that their long drive was about to be over.

Veronica leaned her arm out the open window and let the sun shine on her face. "It's everything like I remembered. The smell, the sounds, the sights ..."

"Right? That's exactly how I felt when I first came down this summer. It had been years since I'd been back to Ocean City," Lauren said as she made a left onto Bay Avenue, which eventually turned into Bay Road.

Minutes later, they arrived in front of Lauren's house. "We're here ... finally," Lauren said, hopping out of the truck and slamming the door behind her.

Veronica got out with her and glanced at her phone. "Dan landed an hour ago in Atlantic City. He's on his way here in a rideshare. Should be arriving any minute now."

"Perfect timing," Lauren said as she walked up the steps to the front door and unlocked it. "You can use the bathroom downstairs, and I'll use the one upstairs," Lauren said, pointing towards the kitchen.

"You read my mind," Veronica said as she bolted towards the back of the house.

Five minutes later, they were both standing on the porch, surveying the neighborhood together.

"To the left is my neighbor Erin and her husband, John. They're great. They have a boat, which is fun. To the right is Matt's house," Lauren said, glancing in that direction. "Doesn't look like he's home yet though."

Veronica plopped down on a cushioned seat on the porch. "It's still so wild to me that you live next to the guy you're dating. What happens if you break up? That would be awkward."

Lauren laughed. "I'm not even going to think about any of that right now."

Just then, an old rattling Chevrolet Impala with dark-tinted windows pulled up in front of the house. After a minute, the door opened, and out stepped Dan.

"Hi, hon!" Veronica yelled as she waved from the porch.

Dan walked up the steps with his luggage, gave Veronica a kiss, and watched as his driver took off. "That was *the* worst rideshare experience of my life. Hands down. I didn't think I was going to make it here."

Lauren widened her eyes. "Oh no. What happened?"

Dan took a deep breath and composed himself. "The driver I booked was twenty minutes late. OK, fine. I can handle that. We finally get on the road, and I kid you not, his side mirror just falls right off as he's driving. I watch it happen with my own eyes. The driver shrugs it off. That's not even the worst of it." Veronica rubbed Dan's back as he continued on. "We get on the Atlantic City Expressway, hit some slow traffic, and he reaches for something on the floor of the passenger seat and rear-ends the car in front of us. Luckily, we weren't going very fast, so it was a minor fender bender."

"This is sounding very dangerous. I should have asked my parents to pick you up. They would have been glad to. I didn't even think about it," Lauren said, feeling awful.

Dan shook his head. "Honestly, I didn't even think of that

either, but next time I'll take you up on that. However, the story gets even worse. After he rear-ends the car, instead of pulling over to exchange insurance information, he takes off down the shoulder of the expressway, like at full speed. That's when I started yelling at him, telling him to slow down and get back on the road."

Veronica stopped rubbing Dan's back and stared at him. "You had this wacko drive you all the way to Ocean City after that? You should have told him to get off at the next exit and drop you at a public place and we'd come get you. I can't believe how scary this is all sounding."

Dan laughed. "I *did* tell him that, and, well, he did drop me off at the next exit … in a CVS parking lot. That's when I called another rideshare to come get me, which leads me to this guy who just drove away. He drove safely, but there was so much trash in that car. It was disgusting, but even with the trash, I was grateful I was out of the last guy's car. Anyway, I'm here. Let me see this fixer-upper," he said, pulling a tape measure out of his suitcase.

Veronica and Lauren stood with their mouths open, still digesting everything Dan had just told them before they followed him inside.

Dan walked around the foyer, then glanced around the house, tapping his tape measure on his leg. "I'm willing to bet some pretty nice wood floors are under this old carpet."

Lauren nodded. "That's what I'm hoping."

Veronica glanced at the little black-and-white television and the white wicker living room furniture. "Oh my gosh, this aesthetic reminds me so much of one of the beach houses we rented as a kid."

Lauren nodded. "Yep. That's all getting donated. Luckily, I was the one who got the couch and chairs in the divorce. He didn't want them."

Veronica walked into the dining room, eyeing the little table with mismatched chairs and the piano in the corner as

Dan measured the doorway of the kitchen. "What about all of this?"

"Getting donated. Well, the piano stays. I need to hire someone to come tune it," Lauren said as she turned to Dan, who was standing with his arms crossed, staring at the kitchen. "What are you thinking?"

Dan rubbed his hands together as Veronica stood next to him. "Well, I haven't seen the rest of the house, but this kitchen needs some updating." He walked over to the Formica backsplash. "See this," he said, tugging on the backsplash. "It's rotting. I could break this off easily with one hand right now. The countertops and cabinets look a little on the newer side, though. However, this linoleum flooring is peeling and should be replaced with tiles, which I can do."

"My gosh, this house is going to cost me a fortune. Maybe I didn't make the right decision," Lauren said, starting to feel anxiety creep up.

Dan cut in. "Look, if you have money for the supplies, I'll do the work for free. That will cut the cost down substantially."

Lauren glanced at Veronica. "I can't have you do that. It wouldn't be right. I'd have to pay you somehow. Plus, when will you have *time*?"

Dan smirked as he put his arm around Veronica. "I think I can make time since we're here for a week or two. Pay us with food and your friendship."

Veronica glanced at Dan and smiled. "Did I not marry the most amazing man ever?"

Lauren reached out and hugged them both at the same time. "You guys are the absolute best."

Dan cleared his throat. "Let's see the rest of the house. I need to see if there's anything else that needs to be done soon."

Lauren led the way upstairs. "The bathroom is somewhat newly remodeled, and the bedrooms seem OK. Not sure there's much to do up here."

Dan looked down. "Except this carpet also has to go."

"And I could help spruce these bedrooms up a bit. Maybe some new paint? Rearrange some furniture. Find some things to hang on walls," Veronica said as she opened a door to one of the bedrooms.

"You have great taste in style. I was hoping you'd give me some input on how to spruce this house up. You guys are getting me excited." Lauren smiled.

Dan headed down the stairs. "Let's get this truck unpacked before dark. That way, we can get that finished and hopefully, get some dinner."

Lauren walked behind them, then paused as they approached the porch. "Wait, did you say you were staying a week or two? Was I hearing things?"

Veronica nodded. "Yes. It's our little surprise. I'll still be able to work remotely on certain days, and so will Dan since he doesn't have to be on his job site right now."

"So, you're staying with me?" Lauren asked.

"We are for a few days, but after that, I booked a room at a local inn for Veronica and I."

"You did? You floor me, Daniel Charles," Veronica said as she kissed him on the cheek.

* * *

"How many cushioned chairs do you need?" Dan asked jokingly while hauling the third one inside.

Lauren laughed as she walked towards the truck. "They pair nicely with the wraparound couch. Plus, they have that vintage feel with the gold velvet fabric."

Veronica nodded as she carried a rattan table lamp. "You've always had impeccable taste."

"And you, the artist, have always had an eye for beauty." Lauren smiled as she grabbed a box of books from the back of the truck. She paused for a moment, noticing Matt had just pulled his Jeep into his driveway.

Veronica and Dan walked out of the house and towards the truck together, both stopping in front of Lauren to peer over at the Jeep.

"Is that him?" Veronica asked excitedly.

Lauren nodded. "It is. He must have just finished work." She started walking with the box of books. "We should probably quit staring. I don't want him to feel awkward."

It was too late. Matt had stepped out of the Jeep with his things, and Veronica was waving. "Hi, Matt!"

Lauren felt herself growing red with embarrassment as she walked inside, set the books down in the corner of the foyer, then ducked into the bathroom behind the kitchen.

"Dan had the worst rideshare experience to date. I think he's scarred from ever using one again," Veronica said as she stepped inside the foyer holding a box of dishes.

Dan laughed. "She's probably right. I'd rather find a private cab company next time."

Then came Matt's voice. "Well, I'll give you my number, and I'll pick you up the next time you're in town."

"Thanks, man," Dan said as he and Matt lowered the table they carried onto the floor of the dining room, seemingly becoming fast friends.

"Hey, Lauren!" Veronica yelled. "Where are you?"

Lauren remained quiet as she stood in the bathroom, deciding if she was ready to come out yet. *Why am I acting like this?* she thought to herself. *I feel like a teenager who's afraid to face my crush. This is so silly.* She looked in the mirror and fixed her hair, then opened the bathroom door to all three of them standing in the kitchen staring at her.

"Oh hi, guys," Lauren said as she joined them in the kitchen. "Hey, Matt! How was work?"

Matt stared at Lauren and smiled. "The store was busy in the morning, then slow for the rest of the day. Besides that, I'm glad you made it safely back to Ocean City."

Lauren felt her heart warm over. "Me too. I got Veronica

back in one piece. Plus all my stuff. I feel accomplished. By the way, I guess you've already formally met my friends Veronica and Dan?"

Dan nodded. "Yep. We did all our introductions already. You missed it."

"So, is there anything else I can help bring inside?" Matt asked.

Veronica shook her head. "That's everything. The dining room table and chairs were the last of it."

"Thank you so much, guys. I appreciate the help," Lauren said.

Dan put his hand on Matt's shoulder. "Did Lauren tell you I'm going to be doing a little remodeling work while we're here?"

Matt's eyes widened as he looked at Lauren then Dan. "No. You do construction?"

Dan nodded. "Sure do. Run a construction business up north. I know my stuff."

Matt crossed his arms. "Oh yeah? How about that. What are you thinking of doing? Do you need an extra pair of hands? I could find some time."

Dan breathed a sigh of relief. "Man, I definitely could use some help if you're willing. I'm ripping up the carpets and redoing some of the kitchen as of now."

Matt rubbed his chin in thought. "This could be fun. I'll finagle some free time."

Veronica glanced at Lauren. "And tomorrow maybe you and I can go pick out paint colors and all that."

Lauren started feeling overwhelmed. "My gosh, this is going to be a lot of work. Are you sure you can do it?" she asked Dan.

Dan nodded. "Yes. Don't worry about me. I love this stuff. It brings me joy, even if it's hard, dirty work."

Matt piped in. "Are you guys hungry?"

Everyone nodded, feeling exhausted.

"Come over to my place, where it's less cluttered. I'll whip something up for dinner," he said, smiling at Lauren.

"Lead the way," Dan said as he put his arm around Matt's shoulders and they headed out the front door while chatting away.

Veronica and Lauren stayed towards the back, giggling to each other. "Look at them. Born to be best friends," Veronica said, shaking her head.

Lauren sighed happily as she watched Matt and Dan walk down the sidewalk towards Matt's. "This is just too funny."

"So, Matt knows how to cook?" Veronica asked.

"You know, I don't know. We've only gone out to eat so far. I guess we'll find out," she said as they walked onto Matt's porch and through the front door.

Veronica's eyes widened when she saw the framed scenic photographs and gorgeous surf-inspired paintings all over the walls. She glanced into the living room to see a beautifully stylish setup. "Wow," she said to Lauren.

Lauren looked around at all the well-cared-for houseplants positioned perfectly by the windows and the tan leather couch with hunter-green throw pillows in the center of the room. "It's great, isn't it?"

"I've seen this decorating style in magazines before but never in person. I believe this is called bohemian meets jungle. This man knows his stuff. I'm thoroughly impressed," Veronica said as she studied the little trinkets on the bookshelves by the fireplace.

"You have a similar decorating style, no?" Lauren asked as she walked to the corner of the room, where a vintage sideboard held a record player and records on top of it.

Veronica shrugged. "Sort of. We both have an artsy style, but mine is more of a maximalist style. I'd make an entire wall a gallery of different framed photographs and paintings."

Just then, Matt and Dan walked into the living room,

holding beers. "Would you two like some beer or wine?" Matt asked.

"Some red wine if you have it." Veronica nodded at Lauren.

"Perfect, I'll go grab it," Matt said as he headed to the kitchen.

Dan stood there drinking his beer and rocking back and forth on the balls of his feet. "So, dinner is going to be good. Matt gave me the rundown."

"Really? Care to share?" Lauren asked.

"He's making barbecue baked chicken breasts, baked potatoes, and roasted veggies. We've decided he's going to show me his cooking tricks and I'm going to school him on remodeling," Dan said proudly.

Matt walked back into the room with the glasses of red wine and handed them to Veronica and Lauren. "You two relax. Dinner should be ready in about an hour," he said as he smiled at Lauren.

Veronica waited for the guys to head out of the room. "Girl. This man is unreal. I'm so excited for you," she whispered.

"It almost feels too good to be true," Lauren whispered back.

CHAPTER FIVE

The next morning, upbeat dance music played as Dan worked on ripping up the old green carpet and the padding underneath it in the foyer. "Lauren! Come look," he yelled as he got the first glimpse of what was under it all.

Lauren and Veronica came bounding down the steps.

"How does it look?" Lauren asked eagerly.

Dan pointed. "Gorgeous dark hardwood floors. They need to be refinished since they've been under this carpeting for so many years. I'll get to that after I get everything pulled up. I think I might need to use your moving truck to lug all this carpet and padding to the dump though."

"Whatever you need. Just let me know. I'm so happy there are hardwood floors under there," Lauren said excitedly as she knelt down to touch the floor.

Dan nodded, then turned the music up louder and went back to pulling up more carpet.

Veronica glanced around at the old furniture that came with the house. "You don't want any of this stuff, right?"

Lauren shook her head. "No, definitely not. Should we put it on the curb?"

Veronica nodded. "Let's do that now. Maybe people will

take it, and we can donate what's left. Then, let's get out of here and go on an adventure."

"Who's going to want all of this?" Lauren laughed.

"You'd be surprised," Veronica said as she lifted a white wicker chair and carried it out the front door.

* * *

After picking out paint colors, cabinet hardware, and tiles for the kitchen floor and backsplash, Lauren decided to give Veronica the tourist treatment—a jaunt around the beach town.

"So, this is it. The Ocean City Boardwalk," Lauren said as the sun pounded on them from above while they walked the boards.

"Gosh, it hasn't changed much from what I remember as a kid. I love that," Veronica said as she looked out towards the ocean. "The beach is packed today."

Lauren stopped and lowered her sunglasses to get a better look. "It is. It looks like the Fourth of July out here. I wonder what's going on?"

Veronica walked to the railing and leaned on it, then Lauren followed. Soon enough, tons of other people had done the same.

"What is going on? What is everyone looking at?" Lauren asked, completely bewildered.

A man next to them overheard and pointed to the sky just as a loud jet flew towards them. "The airshow is today."

"No way! I've always wanted to see this," Lauren said as she saw another jet approach, then fly past them.

They watched old military planes zoom past and then a bunch of stunt pilots put on a nail-biting performance in the sky.

It was getting hot in the crowd that had accumulated around them, so they slipped out and started walking again.

"Wanna grab a coffee?" Veronica asked.

Lauren glanced over at Ocean City Coffee Company. "Yes, and we've arrived at the perfect spot."

Minutes later, they had their coffees and were in bliss as they stopped inside different stores, did some shopping, then popped out again to catch another airshow performance.

They walked along the boardwalk, happily soaking it all in, when Lauren stopped in her tracks.

"What's wrong?" Veronica asked.

Lauren shook her head. "I ... thought I saw something. That was strange."

"Saw what?"

Lauren waved her hand dismissively. "Oh, nothing. I think these sunglasses are distorting my vision somehow," she said, taking them off and wiping the lenses with her shirt.

They made their way to Shriver's and stepped inside into the air-conditioning.

"I could shop all day in here," Veronica said as she looked through the glass cases of homemade fudge.

"It's truly the best. I love the rocky road fudge with the marshmallows and walnuts," Lauren said as she strolled by some salt water taffy.

Veronica glanced around the store, her gaze stopping on a person walking by outside on the boardwalk. She shook her head and continued to shop. "You know, Lauren. I think my eyesight might be going too."

Lauren laughed. "Well, now I feel a little better."

They bought two pounds of fudge and stuffed it into one of their shopping bags as they headed back onto the boardwalk.

Five minutes into walking, sweat poured off Lauren's forehead, and the air was so humid and thick that it felt hard to breathe. "Septembers as a kid felt more like fall than summer, no? Am I imagining that? I don't remember it ever feeling this hot and humid."

"I agree. It feels like August still. Can we find some air-conditioning again maybe?" Veronica asked, scanning the rest of the stores.

Lauren pointed. "How about some Haunted Golf?"

Veronica nodded. "It does say air-conditioned on the sign. I'm sold."

They walk into the haunted-themed mini golf establishment, paid for their tickets, grabbed golf clubs and neon-colored golf balls, and put their bags down to play the first hole.

Veronica hit the ball, and it went clear into the second hole's area, where two people were already playing. "So sorry. It's been a while since I've played," she said, hurrying over to get her ball off their green.

Lauren laughed as Veronica walked back. "We need a practice round before we begin, I think."

"You think?" Veronica said while playfully rolling her eyes. "I'm about to accidentally take people out all over the course with this golf ball."

Lauren looked throughout the crowded indoor space full of haunted props such as chandeliers and ghosts and skeletons with black lights shining on them. Then, she squinted and watched as a man at the back of the room finished hitting his golf ball into the hole, picked it up, then walked into the next room. "Veronica …" Lauren said as she stood in thought.

"Hey, are you guys finished here?" a man asked behind them.

Veronica, who was busy looking at her phone, threw the phone into her purse and picked their bags up off the ground. "Yes, we are. So sorry," she said as she hurried to the next hole with Lauren.

Lauren set her ball down on the tee box and leaned on her golf club. "Veronica, I feel like I'm going crazy. I keep seeing Steven."

Veronica dropped her mouth open after she smacked her club down. "Me too. Are we going crazy?"

Lauren bit her lip as she swung her golf club and hit her ball right into the hole. "We must be. Maybe the heat has made the sweat drip into our eyes? There's no way he'd be in Ocean City. He's not from here; he has no friends or family here. In fact, he always talked about how much he hated New Jersey whenever we came down to visit my family and friends."

Veronica swatted her ball at the hole but missed by a foot. "But for both of us to see him seems a little odd."

Lauren shrugged. "He must have a doppelgänger then. There isn't another explanation."

Veronica tapped her ball again, this time getting it into the hole. She picked up the green ball and studied it. "Let me ask you this. Does he know you are in Ocean City?"

Lauren shook her head. "He shouldn't. I never told him what my plans were after we separated. We only conversed to go over the house selling and dividing up our assets during the divorce. Besides that, I was pretty private with him because I didn't trust him anymore."

Veronica nodded, then looked up to see they had a line of people waiting. "We have to hurry this up. We're holding the whole place up," she said while grabbing Lauren's hand and pulling her to the next hole.

* * *

"So, this is Chipper's," Lauren said as she and Veronica walked through the front door into the empty restaurant.

"It's incredible. Look how vintage and quaint it is!" Veronica said as she walked around, eyeing the wall of autographed photos of celebrities standing with her grandparents. "Wow. They've had so many famous people come through here."

Lauren smiled as she flipped on the switch for the overhead

lights. "My grandparents were very proud of those photos. A lot of athletes came through here too. Everyone wanted to try the famous cinnamon rolls."

"This place is a piece of history. I see why it's so important to the family," Veronica said, taking a seat on the red stool at the counter.

Lauren sat next to her. "It is. But it was also a big fiasco this summer. My parents, who are retired, took over the restaurant, and quickly found it was too much for them. They almost sold to a deceptive man who wanted to level the place to the ground and build something else. Matt was the one who alerted me to what was going on. So to save the business, I decided to take it over."

"Wow … what's next?" Veronica asked, as she looked out the windows at the ocean in the distance.

Lauren sighed. "That's the million-dollar question. Normally, Chipper's is closed during the offseason. That's how it's always been. Now, I have to spend the next two weeks, while the restaurant is closed, to decide if I'm going to reopen for the fall, winter, and spring or wait until May."

"That's a tough decision. Do you feel obligated to try and keep it open for your staff?" Veronica asked as she eyed the vintage Anchor Hocking coffee mugs in colors of orange, green, blue, and yellow stacked under the coffee machine.

Lauren shook her head. "No. They're used to being off during the offseason since most of them have been working at Chipper's for years. Also, we have a lot of servers who have gone back to college already. Honestly, I haven't even brought up the fact that I was thinking of staying open in the offseason to anyone but my friends and family. So, for all I know, I may not have anyone available to work. They probably have other things lined up."

Veronica nodded. "Makes sense. How will you make money to get by though?"

Lauren took a deep breath. "Good question. I have an

extensive background working in events, but I don't even know how I could incorporate that down here. I'd either have to start from scratch with my own company or find somewhere hiring, but it's a pretty niche field. It's not like when you're a teacher looking for a teaching job and there's all these schools in nearby towns to apply to. It's different. A lot of work in that field is through word of mouth."

"I'm sure you'll figure it out. You're very resourceful." Veronica smiled.

"Gosh, I hope so. I have a house to pay for now. I have to figure this all out quick. By the way, I have something I want to show you," Lauren said, standing up and walking through the kitchen. "Follow me."

Veronica followed Lauren through the storage closet in the kitchen and then into a dark and chilly space beyond a doorway. Lauren flicked on the lights, revealing a store frozen in time.

"Where are we? I feel like you just led me to Narnia or something," Veronica said with widened eyes as she peeked inside boxes on shelves.

"This is the little store my grandparents owned that was attached to the restaurant. They shut it down in the nineties and did absolutely nothing with it. They never sold off any of the items for sale. They just locked the door one day and never reopened," Lauren said as she led Veronica down the aisle full of party plates, napkins, and centerpieces.

"I guess the restaurant was bringing in more than enough income that they didn't *have* to care about it, I'm assuming?" Veronica asked as she picked up a pack of birthday paper plates with Garfield on them.

"That's what my parents said, but who knows. It's so weird that they didn't even bother to have a big sale to recoup their money on all of this stock, you know?"

"Well, they blacked out all the windows, I see. It doesn't seem they had any intention of ever reopening," Veronica said, pointing towards the front door and the wall of windows beside it. "Do you think they wanted to expand the restaurant out into the store?"

Lauren widened her eyes. "I think you're onto something there. Maybe that was the plan, but I guess we'll never know. My parents weren't too involved with the restaurant back them. They had their own lives and family, so that very well could have been the case, and we just didn't know it at the time. My grandparents were also very stubborn. It was their way or no way. So, my parents tried to stay out of it."

Veronica picked up a tiny plastic baby in a carriage. "Cake topper?"

Lauren laughed and shrugged. "Beats me. You will find the most random things in here."

Veronica tossed the carriage back into the box. "Do you think you're going to reopen the store?"

Lauren nodded. "Definitely. Not until next spring or summer, but I'd like to sell off all this stuff. Now, will I restock it with new items? Probably not."

"Do you feel like it would be too much to focus on two separate businesses?" Veronica asked.

"Oh, for sure. Though, you see people do it all the time. Those small liquor stores attached to seafood restaurants ... I'm pretty sure those are the same owners, but they have a lot of employees and a whole system down. I think I'd rather focus on the restaurant. Keep it a small operation," Lauren said as she switched off the lights and led them out of the store and through the kitchen.

"We should get back to Dan to see if he needs anything. He's probably wondering where we've been all this time," Veronica said as they stepped out of the front door.

Lauren locked the restaurant up. "I think Matt went over to help him. He wasn't working at Jungle Surf today, which is why I didn't take you there. I want him to be there when you see it. He knows so much about the different surfboards, apparel, plants, and books that he sells. It's truly fascinating," she said as she glanced over at her car parked on the street. Her eyes were immediately drawn to a vehicle passing by.

"What are you looking at?" Veronica asked, craning her neck to see down the street.

Lauren shook her head. "Nothing. I think my mind is playing tricks on me again."

"Did you see Steven?" Veronica asked. "I swear that guy has so many look-alikes."

"I just saw his car. A white Subaru Outback, but there are tons of those cars around. It's just weird that I keep getting reminded of him today. Maybe going back to Vermont and seeing him at the restaurant wasn't good for me. This is all so weird," Lauren said as they made their way to her car.

Veronica shook her head. "He's not my ex, and I was reminded of him today too. That can't be a coincidence."

CHAPTER SIX

"I know this color can be boring, but look how the white paint brightens up this dark room," Veronica said as she ran the paint roller down Lauren's bedroom wall.

Lauren held her paint brush and stepped back to get a better look. "It's night and day. I want this throughout the whole house. It's time to get rid of these dark-green walls and old peeling wallpaper."

Veronica nodded and went back to painting. "I think that will be a good choice. You can decorate the walls and rooms plenty to add color."

"True. Maybe we can go to some thrift and antique stores and find some neat things to hang," Lauren said as she dunked her brush in the paint and swiped it along the window trim.

Downstairs was noisy with Dan sanding the floors after having ripped up all the old carpet in the entire house.

A knock came at the bedroom door, startling Veronica and Lauren. Lauren turned to see Matt standing there, leaning on the door frame with one of his hands in his jeans pocket.

"Did I scare you?" he asked with a smile.

"Yes, you surely did," Veronica blurted as she dipped her roller in the white paint.

"I thought I'd check in to see how it's going before I rush off to the store. My mom offered to help out at Jungle Surf, but she hasn't remembered anything I've told her about working the register," he said with a chuckle.

Lauren smiled. "It's going great. We're painting all the walls white throughout the house. I'm thinking of taking the curtains down and adding bamboo blinds and getting some area rugs to put over the hardwood floors. By the way, I heard you helped Dan out yesterday …"

"I did. We got all the carpet ripped out and taken to the dump in record time. Had a couple beers afterwards and some pizza on the back deck. It was, honestly, quite a bonding and learning experience. Funny enough, I enjoyed doing it," he said as he reached out to nudge Lauren's waist.

Veronica stood up. "Well, Dan went on and on about you afterwards. How you had him laughing for hours. It made the job go faster and easier, that's for sure. We all thank you."

"Yes, we do," Lauren said as she caught his eye and smiled.

Matt and Lauren stared at each other for a few lingering seconds before he snapped out of it. "I've got to go before my mom has a meltdown. I had a friend who owns the store next door go over to help her ring a customer up, but who knows when the next customer will need to pay. Gosh, there might be one right now. I'll talk to you later, Lauren," Matt said as he grabbed her hand, squeezed it, then hurried downstairs.

Veronica waited a moment, then glanced at Lauren with a wide smile. "He likes you. There's no doubt about that."

Lauren blushed, then heard a cell phone ringing. "Is that my phone?" she asked while searching the room. "Where did I put it?"

"Sounds like it's somewhere on the bed," Veronica said, pointing.

Lauren reached under a pillow and pulled it out, her stomach dropping when she saw the caller. "Oh no."

"Who is it?" Veronica asked.

"Steven. I'm not answering," Lauren said, tossing her phone onto the bed.

Veronica stood up and stared at the ringing phone. "Well, now I want to know why he's calling. Maybe he'll leave a message."

They both stared at the phone together, waiting to see if a voicemail notification popped up. It never did.

Lauren shrugged. "See? He probably accidentally hit my number. If it was important, he would have left a message."

Just then, Dan turned off the sander downstairs, and then they heard a knock at the door. Lauren and Veronica stared at each other, wondering if the other was thinking the same thing. They stood in silence, listening to Dan's footsteps as he walked to the front door and opened it.

Lauren stood frozen at the sound of voices talking, but Veronica got up to peek down the steps.

"Who is it?" Veronica asked Dan, who was busy talking to someone through the screen door that she couldn't see.

Dan, not hearing her, continued to converse with the person.

Lauren peeked out the bedroom window to look down at the street. The roof over the porch obscured her view of whoever was at the front door, but she could see a blue SUV with New York plates parked across the street.

Dan finished talking then shut the door, glancing up at Veronica with a bouquet of red roses in his arms. "It was someone delivering flowers. He saw I was sanding floors and wanted to ask me about it. That's all. By the way, tell Lauren there are some flowers here for her."

Lauren, overhearing, walked downstairs with Veronica. She took the roses from Dan and buried her nose in them. They smelled incredible. "Did he say who they were from?"

Dan shook his head. "No, he didn't. Is there a card anywhere?"

Lauren looked inside and outside the bouquet. "Nope."

Just then, there was another knock at the door. This time Lauren opened it, while holding her roses.

Her stomach dropped.

"Hi, Lauren," Steven said.

Veronica and Dan stood ten feet behind Lauren, absolutely stunned.

"What are you doing here?" Lauren asked, feeling more uncomfortable by the minute.

"Well, I called—" Steven started.

Lauren cut him off. "That's why you called? To tell me you were in Ocean City?"

Steven nodded. "Essentially, yes. I see you got my flowers."

Lauren stared at the flowers in her arms. "These are from *you*? How did you get my address?"

"I probably shouldn't say. I did some detective work," Steven said.

Lauren squinted. "You did some detective work? This sounds like a nice way of saying stalking. I don't really understand why you are here and why you are sending me, your ex-wife, roses. This is all extremely inappropriate."

Steven took a deep breath, then looked behind Lauren to see Dan and Veronica standing there. "Oh hi, guys. Didn't see you there."

Veronica and Dan stared back. "Steven, you should probably go," Dan said sternly as he crossed his arms.

"Look, I just need a chance to talk to Lauren. I haven't stopped thinking about her since I saw her at Vincenzo's the other night," Steven said as he glanced up at Lauren.

Before Lauren could say anything, Veronica chimed in. "Steven, you may have noticed we were at Vincenzo's with her, and you were with my old hairstylist. You know, the one you *cheated* on Lauren with."

Steven hung his head. "Right. Yes, that was us, but that's over. We aren't together anymore."

Lauren rolled her eyes. "Well, that's a shame. You two

seemed perfect for each other. I wish you well, Steven, but don't bother me again. We are divorced and done. I have started a new life here in Ocean City. I've moved on."

"It's about six and a half hours to South Burlington. You'll make it home before dark if you leave now," Veronica said as she leaned in front of Lauren to shut the front door.

They all peeked out of the front window and watched as Steven got into the blue SUV and drove off down the street.

Dan snarled, "I can't believe the nerve of that guy. I really can't. Who does he think he is? Some Casanova who's going to come back into your life after he wronged you and sweep you off your feet?"

Lauren laughed. "That's not happening. What am I going to do with these roses now?"

Veronica grabbed them. "These roses did nothing wrong. They're going in a vase."

* * *

"This is it. Dock's Oyster House," Matt said as he switched places with the valet outside the Atlantic City eatery.

"We love it here. We usually arrive early for the happy hour seating at the bar," Joe, Lauren's father, said as he held hands with Lauren's mother, Nancy.

"Same for us, right, John?" Erin smiled at her husband as Lauren, Matt, Dan, and Veronica followed them into the busy restaurant.

Happy hour was just about to end, and the counter was jam-packed. Luckily, they had a reservation for a party of eight and were seated promptly at a long table. Lauren and Matt sat next to each other in the middle, staring at their menus.

"How did today go? Did you get more work done on the house?" Matt asked Lauren, Veronica, and Dan.

Dan widened his eyes. "Well ..."

Lauren cut in. "We finished painting a few more rooms, and Dan got most of the sanding done, right?"

Dan nodded. "Correct. May do a little more tomorrow, but I think it's just about ready for the stain and sealant."

Joe and Nancy and John and Erin sat at the end of the table and were in their own discussion when Joe caught wind of the flooring talk and glanced at Dan. "You know your stuff, huh?"

Dan shrugged and smiled. "I know a thing or two. I run a construction business up north."

"Well, we thank you for helping Lauren out with the house. We can't wait to see the finished product," Nancy said.

Just then, the server showed up to take their drink order, and they were soon back to their conversations.

Lauren looked up at Matt. "Were you able to get everything figured out at the store? I know your mom was working out some issues with the register."

Matt laughed. "Oh jeez. Yeah. There was a line of people by the time I got there. Luckily, they were very patient, and my mom kept them entertained with her stories while she waited for me to arrive. I can't ask for better customers. Last thing I need is people being rude to my mom. It's something I worry about with her filling in."

"I totally understand," Lauren said, loving the fact that he cared so much about his mother.

Erin tilted her head to see the rest of the table. "Matt, did you send that gorgeous bouquet of roses to Lauren? Don't think I didn't notice it when we stopped over before dinner," she said with a wink.

Veronica cleared her throat and stumbled on her words. "The roses. That's right …"

Matt shook his head. "I'd like to take the credit for that, but no, I didn't. Who sent them?" he asked Lauren.

Lauren glanced at Dan and Veronica, looking for an idea

of what to say or how to say it. She was met with blank stares, as they were in the same boat.

"Shockingly, they are from my ex-husband, Steven," she blurted out.

Matt froze. "Your ex-husband?"

Lauren nodded. "He showed up at my door today, and I don't know why."

Nancy squinted. "Hold up. Did you say Steven showed up today? Here in Ocean City ... and at your door?"

"Yes, Mom. It was awful. I have no explanation for it," Lauren said as she glanced at Matt, who looked very confused.

Their drinks arrived, and Lauren took a long swig of her white wine.

Dan took a sip of his beer and cleared his throat. "So, since everyone is wondering. I answered the door since I was downstairs working and Veronica and Lauren were upstairs painting. I know Steven and immediately was shocked to see him. He would not tell us how he found Lauren's address, but apparently, he's here to try and work things out with her."

"Which is not happening," Lauren chimed in.

Erin gasped. "That was him? That guy in the blue SUV parked in front of the house?"

"Yes," Lauren nodded.

"Let me tell you. John and I have seen that SUV drive down our street many times over the past couple of days," Erin said as she nodded at John.

"Morning and night. We were out on the front porch a lot, enjoying the weather, so it was quite odd. We thought maybe someone new moved into the neighborhood with that specific vehicle. It was the only thing that made sense."

"Plus the SUV would always slow down when it got in front of your house, then it would speed up," Erin said, nodding, proud of her detective skills.

Matt glanced at Lauren. "This guy sounds no good. Do you feel safe?"

Lauren nodded. "I do. He never made me feel unsafe during the years we were married, but this is unlike him. I never would have imagined he'd do something as extreme as this."

Veronica cleared her throat. "You know, Lauren, all those times we thought we saw his doppelgänger on the boardwalk? That was probably him."

"Oh, my gosh. You're right. This is so weird, and I'm guessing that blue SUV is a rental. He had a white Subaru the last time I saw him."

Matt rubbed his chin. "Do you need me to talk to this guy?"

Lauren shook her head. "I think we took care of it. I told him I've moved on and to not come around again. I think he got the point. He's probably already back home in Vermont."

"Hopefully," Dan said as he took another sip of his beer.

Veronica's eyes widened as an idea popped in her head. "Lauren. What if he rented the blue SUV on purpose so you wouldn't get suspicious when he drove by all those times?"

Lauren rubbed her temples, feeling stress building up. "OK, this is starting to freak me out. Maybe we should talk about something else," she said, nudging Veronica under the table with her foot.

Veronica glanced at Matt, who was busy looking at the menu. "Right. Yes, well, here's another topic. Dan and I are spending the night at the Breezy Shores Inn tonight and for the rest of the time we're here."

Nancy gasped. "Oh! The Breezy Shores Inn? I hear it's absolutely wonderful there."

Erin rubbed her chin in thought. "The Breezy Shores Inn ... I've heard a thing or two about that place."

Dan smiled. "It has top ratings online. I knew I'd be helping Lauren with the house, so I thought I'd add a little pampering for Veronica while we're here. This way, we can see some other sides of Ocean City too."

"You'll have to come visit us and see what it's like," Veronica said to Lauren.

"For sure. I'd love to see it," Lauren said as she lightly touched Matt's hand. Suddenly, a part of her was mortified that her ex-husband had been such a big topic of discussion at the table that he was sitting at. Was all of this drama going to scare him off?

CHAPTER SEVEN

Lauren stepped out of her car and walked down the sidewalk to get to the Breezy Shores Inn. The inn was large and took up over half the block. It was right on the beach and located on a one-way street, which kept the road on the quiet side, as there wasn't much traffic or even parking spots.

"My gosh. This place is a lot bigger than I remember," Lauren said as she walked along the giant green arborvitaes that bordered the tall stone wall around the entire property of the inn. She finally got to the high white gate and had started to unlatch it when someone opened it from the inside.

"I've got it for you, miss," the worker said as he held the gate open with a smile.

Lauren was taken aback, as she wasn't expecting someone to man the gate at an inn in Ocean City. "Why, thank you. Appreciate it," Lauren said as she nodded and smiled.

As the gate closed, Lauren looked around her, as though she'd just arrived in another country. On the inside of the fencing was one of the most magical courtyards she'd ever seen. There were massive fountains with different sculptures trickling water down, beautiful stone pathways with lush green moss between each stone, patios, arbors with grape vines or ivy growing along them. Then, the stone walls had tangerine, white, and pink climbing roses.

Lauren put a hand on her heart and took a deep breath. This place was absolutely stunning. She walked around the courtyard some more, noticing guests sitting and eating breakfast at some of the tables and chairs. A few had small dogs by their sides, and they all seemed to have their own water bowls. "Pet friendly. I like that," Lauren said to herself.

Suddenly, her phone rang.

"Hey. Are you here?" Veronica asked.

Lauren nodded. "I am. I've been taking in this insane courtyard. I feel like I'm at some exotic resort."

Veronica smiled. "It's great, isn't it? I can't believe Dan was able to book this."

"What do you mean?" Lauren asked. "Is it hard to book?"

Veronica nodded. "It is. He called seconds after someone else cancelled."

Lauren laughed. "Well, this is surely better than staying at my place, especially right now with the huge mess from the floors and painting."

"Come up here. Tell the front desk you're here for me. Room 12," Veronica said, then hung up.

Lauren put her phone in her pocket and saw the door to the inside bordered by ceiling-high windows. She walked in expecting the place to have marble floors and counters and big gold chandeliers, but instead it had black-and-white checkered tile floors and a long wooden counter with milk glass vases full of colorful zinnias. The walls had framed paintings by local artists, and instead of chandeliers, there were hanging Edison bulbs of all sizes and lengths. She was enamored. It felt so chic.

"Can I help you?" a voice asked.

Lauren glanced at the desk to see a woman staring at her. "Yes, I'm here to see a friend. She said to come right up. Room 12, I think it was."

"Oh, that's on the second floor. Just take the stairs and turn right. Should be a few doors down," the woman said.

Lauren headed to the stairs, then to room 12, and before she could knock, the door swung open.

"Oh my, I'm so head over heels for this place, Lauren," Veronica said before turning around. "Hon! We have to give Lauren the tour." She turned back around. "He's on a phone call with work. I probably shouldn't have done that," Veronica said with a giggle as she took Lauren's hand and led her inside.

"Is this a suite?" Lauren asked, somewhat shocked.

"Yes. Surprising, right? I was expecting a studio room layout," Veronica said as she eyed the room. "This is the living room. Great, isn't it?"

Lauren sat on the white chaise, then noticed there were paintings on the walls just like the lobby had. She looked around some more, seeing that the kitchen had black-and-white checkered floors, and there were Edison bulbs hanging above the kitchen counter. "It looks similar to the lobby."

"Right?" Veronica said as she flopped onto the trendy orange couch next to Lauren. "The bathroom is incredible. A tiled steam shower. Heated towel racks. Not one but two sinks, and the largest, fluffiest white towels you've ever seen."

Lauren leaned back on the chaise. "My gosh, this is nothing like I pictured. I guess I'm used to those quaint, adorable inns that have ruffle curtains and old rocking chairs."

"That's exactly what I pictured too—though I don't mind an older inn—but this ... I could live here. Easily," Veronica said as she got up. "Come see the view."

Lauren followed her to the balcony, where Dan was finishing his phone call. "Front-row seats to the ocean. Can't get better than this."

"Hey, Lauren," Dan said as he reached over to give her a hug. "You hungry? We're about to go get breakfast downstairs."

Lauren nodded. "I am, but I'm not a guest here. Can I still grab a bite?"

"Yes, we've already asked. We'll just have to pay for yours, but we've got it. Our treat," Dan said as he walked to the door.

Lauren went to argue about them paying, but didn't have time as they hurried out the door, down the stairs, and out to the courtyard that faced the beach. Instead of roses, green ivy, and stone pathways like the other courtyard, it was bordered by sandy dunes and had the sounds of the ocean, along with a large saltwater pool and lots of tables with umbrellas.

"Is here good?" Dan asked as he pointed to a table.

"Perfect," Veronica said as she sat down.

Lauren took her seat and opened the menu, then peeked over it to see two guys playing horseshoes. Down farther was a pair of couples playing badminton, and past them, she could see firepits, though unlit, as the weather didn't call for them yet.

A joyful server came by. "Hi, everyone. My name is Josie. Can I start you with drinks?"

Dan piped in. "We might be ready to order too," he said looking at Veronica and Lauren.

Lauren quickly scanned the menu to figure out what she wanted. Dan seemed very hungry.

"I'll have the fresh-squeezed orange juice and the crab eggs Benedict," Veronica said.

Lauren nodded. "I'll take the raspberry swirl French toast and coffee."

"And I'll take the steak and eggs with fried potatoes. Oh yeah, a coffee too," Dan said as he handed the server their menus.

They watched the server walk away, then took in the sounds of the ocean, letting it lull them each into a trance.

Lauren took a deep breath. "This feels like a five-star resort. It couldn't have been cheap."

Dan shrugged. "Well, it wasn't cheap, but it wasn't too

pricey either. Honestly, now that we're here, I'm shocked I got it for the price I did."

"It might be because it's offseason already," Veronica said as their drinks arrived.

Dan nodded. "Also, Lauren. Don't think I forgot about the house. Planning to get over there after breakfast. I'm excited to see how the floors look after everything is stained and sealed."

Lauren shook her head. "Dan, don't feel obligated. Take some days off from that. Enjoy your stay here at this exotic inn."

Veronica rolled her eyes. "Trust me. He'd rather be working on your floors. He loves what he does."

"She's right. It's why I do what I do. Even on vacation, I need to be kept busy," Dan said, smiling.

* * *

They finished eating and walked back inside, passing through a long hallway that didn't seem remodeled like the rest of the inn. It looked to have the original wood trim, crown molding, and hardwood floors. They quickly passed what appeared to be a library, which looked very rustic and vintage, and then a large room with the doors propped open. Lauren stopped and stared, watching workers walk back and forth past her with flowers, catering dishes, lighting, and sound equipment. It was bustling.

"Do they do weddings here?" Lauren asked Veronica and Dan.

Veronica thought for a moment. "You know, I think they do. Last night, we saw a huge group of people checking in. Looked like a bridal party perhaps."

Lauren walked into the room, staring at the lighting, then at the arbor at the front of the room, where a person stood on a ladder, trying to decorate it.

"What do you think?" a voice asked behind Lauren's shoulder.

She looked behind her, surprised not to see Veronica or Dan, but instead the woman that had been at the front desk.

Lauren nodded, thinking of what to say. "Looks like a great place to have a wedding, that's for sure."

The woman looked down at her long purple fingernails. "I sure hope so. We just started offering the inn as a wedding spot this month."

"Really? Well, good luck to you ... and to whoever owns the inn," Lauren said as she watched someone walk past her with silk tiger lilies.

"That would be me. I own the inn," the woman said, slightly irritated. "I'm Charlotte, by the way," she said, extending her hand. "Did I see you earlier?"

"I'm Lauren, and yes, I came in to visit some friends. I live here in Ocean City. Newly transplanted."

Charlotte tossed her long red hair behind her shoulder. "What brought you to Ocean City?"

"My parents retired here, and someone needed to take over Chipper's, my grandparents' restaurant," Lauren said as a speaker near them suddenly let out some loud feedback.

Charlotte and Lauren both held their ears.

"The speakers really should be next to the DJ, facing the dance floor, not back in those corners in front of the tables where people are eating," Lauren said as she glanced in that direction.

Charlotte shifted her eyes. "Really? How do you know that?"

Lauren sighed. "Many years of managing events. I worked high-end weddings, corporate events, concerts, festivals, you name it. Our company did it all."

"And now you're here taking over a restaurant .... What a big career shift," Charlotte said as she crossed her arms.

Lauren shrugged. "It is, but a divorce made me want to

60

leave Vermont and try something new. Right now, though, I have to decide if I'm going to keep Chipper's open all year or just seasonally."

"That's quite a decision," Charlotte said as she watched a worker accidentally trip on one of the uplights on the ground. "Do you have any other input about how things are getting set up here?"

Lauren nodded. "Those uplights should face the ceiling and be put along the walls or standing structures. It looks like they are currently pointing at the tables. If you want lighting on the tables, I recommend using Leko lights. They can be either hung from the ceiling or attached to poles that stand on the ground. They're also great for dance floor lighting, as you can just add a gobo to give the light a more textured look.

"Then, the flowers ... Who did you hire?"

Charlotte paused in thought, thoroughly impressed with Lauren's knowledge. "Who did I hire? Oh, someone I found online. My normal florist that does our bouquets around the hotel doesn't do events, so I had to quickly find someone."

Lauren nodded. "It's really best to get a company that regularly does flowers for big events. It takes a lot of manpower, and silk flowers tend to look a little gaudy if not done right," she said pointing to the arbor.

Charlotte glanced in that direction. "You're right. They didn't mention silk flowers. I thought it was all going to be fresh."

Lauren shrugged. "All important details to know in the future for when the inn hosts more events," she said, glancing towards the doorway. "I wonder where my friends went. They were right out in the hall," Lauren said, pointing.

"When I walked in, I saw them heading towards the stairs," Charlotte said, nodding towards the door.

Lauren sighed. "Hopefully, they're not waiting on me. Just know that this place is incredible. I mean, this inn feels like you're in another state—country, even—when you walk through that gate into the courtyard."

Charlotte smiled. "Well, like you, I took over a family business, but I decided to change things up. I had a lot of it remodeled, but also kept some other areas the same."

Lauren's eyes lit up. "I saw the library in passing. It's stunning."

"Only in passing. Oh, come with me. You need to see all of it. It hasn't been touched at all since it was originally built except to fix a few things. The wood floors, the tall wood bookshelves, the dim warm lighting and lamps, the old books, the leather smell. It's divine," Charlotte said, leading Lauren down the hall and into the library.

They entered, and Lauren's eyes widened with delight. It was so cozy, and it was neat seeing guests tucked away in chairs in the corners, reading quietly. "This is so unique. I don't know many inns that have a library."

"It started as my father's personal library, and when it became an inn, he opened it to guests. I come here to get peace and quiet sometimes. It's a nice little escape," Charlotte said as she pulled a mystery book off the shelf and studied the cover.

Lauren took her phone out of her pocket and glanced at the time. "I better go in case my friends are waiting on me. It was so nice meeting you and hearing about the inn."

Charlotte nodded. "Look, Lauren, if you decide to keep Chipper's closed and not reopen it for the year, I may have a job opportunity here at Breezy Shores Inn for you."

That piqued Lauren's interest. "Really? What were you thinking?"

"Well, I'd have you do a background check and all of those employment hiring obligations first, but I've been looking for someone who knows their stuff, and it's been really hard finding that the past year. I can't tell you the number of people I've interviewed," Charlotte said as she rolled her eyes.

"Not one person worked out?" Lauren asked, shocked.

Charlotte shook her head. "The applicants I received were very underqualified. The ones that looked good on paper just didn't do it for me in the interview. I guess I'm picky."

"Well, what would I be doing?" Lauren asked.

"Probably just helping me manage the inn. I could definitely use your help with booking the events and vendors," Charlotte said.

"And this would be until I opened the restaurant back up? I don't think I could do both."

"Yes, we could work that out." Charlotte nodded.

"Well, I need some time to think this over, that's for sure. It might be a couple weeks before I have an answer for you," Lauren said as she started thinking about Chipper's.

"That's totally fine. Just let me know when you know," Charlotte said as they walked out of the library together.

CHAPTER EIGHT

The following day, Lauren and Veronica sat on the beach, relaxing in their chairs.

"Eighty-four degrees in September. I guess this is the locals' summer everyone talks about," Lauren said as she looked around, noticing a lot of couples among them.

Veronica lowered her sunglasses and glanced up and down the beach. "Not a kid in sight. They're all in school, I guess."

"So, I need to tell you what happened yesterday at Breezy Shores Inn," Lauren said as she applied sunblock on her chest and shoulders. "That woman who owns the inn? She offered me a position."

"For real?" Veronica asked, surprised. "That's why you were downstairs so long?"

"Yes, I forgot to mention that after we met back up yesterday. I was scoping out the room where they were setting up the wedding, you know, because of my work experience, and Charlotte, the owner, was impressed with my knowledge."

"Are you going to take it?" Veronica asked as she grabbed Lauren's bottle of sunblock and applied some on her legs and arms.

Lauren sighed and leaned back in her chair. "I don't know.

I told her I need time to make a decision. I still have to figure out what's going on with Chipper's."

"Right. Right. Well, at least you know you have options now. I mean, think about how cool it would be to work at that inn. It's so fancy and upscale," Veronica said.

"It feels more like a boutique hotel than an inn, honestly. It's not the only thing I'm thinking about though ..." Lauren said as she drifted off into thought.

"What else?" Veronica asked as she watched a seagull swoop down on a woman's french fries.

"Matt ... he's been a little distant lately, it feels like. I can't put my finger on it," Lauren said as she watched the same seagull call out to its friends to join him in the french fry theft.

Veronica shrugged. "I'm not seeing that. He's been over a lot helping Dan out with your house. He always seems to be around."

Lauren bit her lip. "Yeah, but emotionally it feels different. He hasn't asked me too much about Steven with everything that's been going on. I guess I kind of expected him to."

"Why would you expect him to?" Veronica asked, confused.

"I've been hoping to have a deep discussion with him about it all. I kind of want him to know where I stand. That I'm completely over that marriage. That there isn't any regret," Lauren said.

"So, tell him!" Veronica blurted out, causing a few couples around them to look in their direction.

Lauren chuckled. "It's not an easy thing to casually bring up in conversation, which is why I'd rather he ask."

"See if he wants to get together tonight. Just you and him. Dan and I will go find something to do," Veronica said.

"I think I will. I'll give him a text later," Lauren said as she noticed flies swarming around them.

Veronica swatted a greenhead fly off of her leg. "Ow! These things bite hard."

Lauren screamed as one bit the top of her foot. "They for sure do. The wind must be bringing them in."

After swatting a bunch more off them, Veronica stood up. "Let's get out of here and go shopping. I can't take these flies anymore."

"Sounds good to me," Lauren said, packing up her stuff.

* * *

Twenty minutes later, Veronica and Lauren were strolling down Asbury Avenue, bags in hand.

"Look at this cute shop," Veronica said, walking inside.

Lauren looked up at the sign, which read Mew to You.

Veronica poked her head out the door. "You have to get in here. It's a cat rescue and a resale store. I think I've found my dream shop."

Lauren followed her inside, glancing at the different items for sale. There were dishes, glasses, purses, books, lamps, and everything else you could think of.

Veronica peeked through a window and saw all of the cats inside. They had a room to themselves where they could sit on cat trees or snuggle in little beds.

"Oh, my heart," Lauren said as she stood next to Veronica and noticed an older tuxedo cat washing its paws while resting in a fuzzy bed.

"I could stand here and watch them play or sleep for hours. How neat is this place?" Veronica said as she stepped away to pick up a green vase.

Lauren walked past the register, and her eyes were immediately drawn to something on the ground in the back. She rushed over and picked it up. "Veronica, come see this!"

Veronica widened her eyes as she saw what Lauren was holding. "A hanging stained-glass window? That would look amazing in your home."

Lauren glanced at it. It was a long windowpane with

purple pansies all throughout. "I'm thinking this would be great over the kitchen window as the sunlight would come through perfectly."

Veronica nodded. "Most definitely. But I need to show you the lamp I found. It's the kind you see over pianos to light the sheet music."

"I would love that," Lauren said as she followed Veronica to the front of the store, where the gold lamp sat. "Oh, that's gorgeous," Lauren murmured as she ran her finger over it.

"I'm buying the lamp for you," Veronica said as she grabbed the lamp and headed to the register. "Next, let's go and find you some area rugs that will pop nicely with the new hardwood floors."

They paid for their items and as they were leaving, Lauren paused and looked back towards the cat room. "I just want to watch the cats one more time."

They put their items in the car and headed back inside to the cat room. Lauren immediately looked for the older cat that she had seen earlier. "There he is."

"You know it's a boy?" Veronica asked, confused.

Lauren laughed. "I don't, but he reminds me of one with that tuxedo of black fur and a white chest."

They watched a female volunteer sit on a chair inside the room, and the cat hopped out of his bed and walked up to her legs and rubbed them.

"He's absolutely adorable," Lauren said as she watched him jump onto the volunteer's lap and settle in.

Veronica smirked. "Thinking about getting a cat?"

"It's on my mind, but right now is not a good time with the big mess in my house. I grew up with cats and have always loved them, but Steven was allergic. Now's my chance to finally have the furry companion I've been dreaming about," Lauren said as she looked longingly at the cat she had her eye on.

* * *

That evening, Lauren and Matt went for a long walk around Ocean City.

"I'm surprised you wanted to come," Lauren said as she smiled at Matt.

"What? For a walk? I love some exercise," Matt said as he smiled back.

Lauren shrugged. "I guess I thought you'd be too exhausted."

Matt nodded. "Well, I am a little. It's more difficult to find good help in the offseason than I originally thought. I feel like I've been working nonstop since summer ended."

"Were sales a little better today at least?" Lauren asked.

Matt sighed. "Honestly, it was dead. I had a few sales, but I spent most of my time sitting on my laptop behind the counter, getting my bookkeeping in order."

"That stinks," Lauren said as they walked through the neighborhoods of Ocean City, lit by streetlamps.

Matt looked up ahead. "There's Starfish Cove Inn."

Lauren squinted her eyes to see. "The one with all of the pretty white string lights on the front porch?"

Matt nodded. "Yes, a buddy of mine runs it."

They heard music in the distance, and as they approached, they saw guests sitting on the porch, enjoying the warm evening temperatures, with a quartet playing Django Reinhardt tunes.

They both stopped in front of the inn, fully embracing how neat it was to have such a bustling, historic inn in the center of town. It was full of beauty, from the big wraparound porch with decorative woodwork and trim to the sage-green siding and steeply pitched roof with gables.

Just then, a voice called out over the music, "Matt! Is that you?"

Matt looked up to the porch to see his friend, Travis, leaning on the front doorway. "It sure is!" Matt said with a chuckle.

"Well, get on up here," Travis said as he motioned with his hand and walked inside the inn.

Matt and Lauren walked up the steps of the porch, now fully immersed among the guests and music. It felt like the coolest place in town.

Travis was back outside, this time holding two drinks complete with mint sprigs and limes on the rim. "Try our homemade mint limeade," he said, handing it to them. "By the way, who's your ... friend?"

Matt smiled. "This is Lauren. She just moved here this summer."

Lauren took a sip of her drink. "It's nice to meet you. By the way, this drink is fantastic. You can tell it's all fresh ingredients."

Travis smiled. "Good! My wife, Kelly, grew the mint herself out back."

"Where is Kelly?" Matt asked. "I feel like I haven't seen her in forever."

Travis sighed. "She's been running the kids to all their practices and rehearsals. It's nonstop these days with the start of school. We usually take turns doing that and working the inn to keep everything running smoothly," he yelled over the loud music before turning to look inside. "How about we go sit on the couch, where it's quieter?"

They went inside, and the interior was just as vintage and charming as the exterior.

Travis pointed to the antique red couch in front of the fireplace. "Have a seat. Let's catch up. Tell me everything."

Matt cracked his knuckles. "Well, let's see. Trying out keeping Jungle Surf open this fall. So far, it doesn't seem like a good decision."

Travis nodded. "That's surprising *and* not surprising. A lot of our business down here is seasonal. It makes it hard being open year-round, that's for sure."

"You guys manage to do pretty good in the offseason," Matt said as he glanced outside at all the guests on the porch.

"We do. Obviously, it's busier for us in the summer, but a lot of people enjoy the beach in the fall, winter, and spring. For one, it's quieter and the rates are cheaper. The older crowd especially enjoys the offseason, from what I've seen. They also have more flexibility since the kids are grown up," Travis said as he grabbed Matt and Lauren's empty glasses and headed to the kitchen to refill them.

Moments later, Travis was back with full glasses of limeade. "So, Lauren ... do you have a job here in Ocean City?"

Lauren sighed. "Well, funny you ask. I took over my parents' restaurant at the end of the summer ..."

Travis cut in. "Oh yeah? Which restaurant?"

"Chipper's," Lauren said as she took a sip of her drink.

Travis's eyes widened. "Chipper's? That's my family's favorite spot in town for breakfast. That place is a gem. Good for you!"

Lauren smiled. "Thank you. I've got days to decide if I'm keeping it open in the offseason or opening it next May, which is what has always been done in the past."

Travis nodded. "That's a tough decision. Chipper's has never been open in the offseason?"

Lauren shook her head. "Not that I know of. So there's really nothing to go by in terms of how it's done in the past. However, it seems another job opportunity has presented itself should I keep it closed till May."

Travis sat on the edge of his seat. "What job?"

"With the Breezy Shores Inn. The owner offered me a position based on my background of working in events," Lauren said as she smiled at Matt.

Matt cleared his throat. "She has friends staying there right now, and when she went to visit, she was blown away by how resort-like it was. I guess the owner was pretty blown away by her too." He chuckled.

Travis's face turned serious as he crossed his arms. "You're talking about Charlotte, the owner, I'm assuming, right?"

"Yes, Charlotte. That's her," Lauren said.

Travis paused in thought for a moment. "Look, I don't know if it's my place to say something. Frankly, speaking on other competitors in town is probably not a good look, but ..."

Matt cut in. "I'm your friend. Whatever you say stays with us."

Travis glanced around the room to make sure nobody was in earshot to overhear. "Fine. Charlotte is a sham. She's known for being terrible to her workers. She'll be nice to your face and then backstab you the second you turn around. Me and the other inn owners in town do not have a good relationship with her."

Lauren widened her eyes. "Really?"

Travis sighed. "Look, I don't want to be the reason you don't take that job, but I feel you should know everything before you commit. That was a family-run inn she took over, and she made it into a mega resort-like complex to try and beat out all competition. Nobody was in competition with her. The rest of us inn owners stay in touch and help each other out, but she wasn't about that way of life. All I can say is things turned nasty really quick."

"I guess I'm just shocked. She seemed so nice and down-to-earth," Lauren said as she glanced at Matt.

"Not surprising. She knows how to schmooze people. She also knows how to be awful to people. Sometimes, you never know who you're going to get. That's what makes her a bad boss to work for," Travis said. "Always having to walk on eggshells."

"This is good information to have," Matt said as he sat up. "What are you thinking, Lauren?"

Lauren bit her lip. "Well, I was really excited about the prospect of having an offseason job should I need it. But I guess that probably won't work out."

"I feel bad. Maybe you should give it a go. Maybe she's changed in the past six months. Who's to say?" Travis said as clapping noises from the guests on the porch filled the room.

"No, I appreciate you telling me this. I think it's important to know for when I make this final decision, and trust me, this information will be factored in."

Matt glanced around the inn. "Personally, I've always preferred these quaint historic inns like Starfish Cove over those fancy upscale ones. It has a certain charm and coziness to it that you don't see in resorts or hotels."

Travis nodded. "It's why we stay in business."

CHAPTER NINE

"So, what is this? A car show?" Lauren asked as she and Matt walked along the sunny boardwalk.

Matt nodded as he stopped in front of a red 1970 Corvette. "The Corvette show. Happens every year. I think this one got pushed back due to the rain last weekend."

"This is pretty neat," Lauren said as they walked between the cars on the boardwalk amongst the crowd.

Matt took a picture of a blue 1996 Corvette. "It is. Ocean City has all kinds of great events throughout the year. Better mark your calendar for next year," he said with a smile.

They walked some more, stopping at times to get pictures with the cars or to look closely at the interior details. When Lauren looked up, she stopped in her tracks and grabbed Matt's hand. "You hungry? Let's go in here," she said while dragging Matt into a pizza shop.

Matt shifted his eyes. "We ate thirty minutes ago. You're hungry already?"

Lauren paused in thought. "Well, maybe I'm just thirsty. I'm going to get a drink. What would you like?"

Matt shrugged. "I'll take a bottle of water, I guess."

Lauren ordered their drinks, Matt paid, and they took a

seat at an empty table in the shop. She took a few sips, then looked out the window.

Matt took a swig of water from his bottle. "So ... are you ready to leave? We can walk with these drinks."

Lauren craned her neck to peer out the front window. "Um ... yeah. Let's head out. I just needed to rest for a minute. I, uh, felt some weird cramp in my leg. I think it's gone," she said as she got up and led the way back onto the boardwalk.

Five minutes later, Lauren's eye caught on something again. This time, she took her baseball cap out of her purse, threw it on her head, and lowered it until her eyes were hidden, then ducked behind an older-model black Corvette.

Matt stood next to her. "What are you doing?"

Lauren kept herself lowered near the ground. "I'll tell you in a minute. Is that guy in the bright-yellow shirt still standing by that white Corvette up ahead?"

Matt looked down the boardwalk. "Well, yeah. Oh ... wait ... he's heading this way now. What's going on, Lauren?"

Lauren promptly stood up and pulled Matt into the Johnson's Popcorn line, positioning their backs to the boardwalk. "My ex-husband is still in town apparently. That's him in the yellow shirt. I can't believe this."

Matt glanced back at Steven, who didn't seem to notice them as he studied another Corvette nearby. "You should have just told me that. Why don't we leave then?"

Lauren bit her lip as they moved up in line. "I didn't want to tell you. I feel like all this drama with my ex-husband looks bad. I still can't believe he showed up here in Ocean City. What is he doing? Taking a week-long vacation now?"

Matt laughed. "Maybe. Lots of people like Ocean City this time of the year."

Lauren chuckled, loving that Matt made her laugh during this strange moment in time. "Well, I guess we're getting caramel popcorn to go. Might as well get one of these huge buckets," she said as they moved up to the front of the line.

As they walked away with their bucket of caramel popcorn, Matt put his arm around Lauren and kissed her on the head. "You're beautiful."

Lauren smiled. "And you're handsome. Did you want to stop at Jungle Surf?"

Matt nodded. "I was just going to bring that up. I have a new employee who started today—Will. I gave him the whole rundown and training yesterday. Let's see how he's doing."

They headed to Jungle Surf, where a few customers were shopping and reggae music softly played over the speakers. It was calm, and everything seemed peaceful.

Matt looked around. "Where's Will?"

Lauren looked towards the counter, noticing it was empty. "Maybe he's in the bathroom or in the back getting something?"

"Probably," Matt said as he fixed the positioning of a few books for sale.

A female customer came up to Lauren. "Do you work here?"

Lauren shook her head. "I don't, but he does," she said, pointing to Matt.

"What can I help you with?" Matt asked.

The customer pointed to a couple of her friends standing near the dressing rooms. "My friends and I have been waiting to use the dressing room for ten minutes. This guy said he'd unlock them for us but never returned."

Matt glanced at Lauren with a confused look, then headed behind the counter to get the key. "Sorry about that. I'll get that open right away for you all."

Lauren felt the tension building in the shop from Matt's stress. She stood by a rack of dresses and pulled one out to get a better look when Matt walked up to her. "Something is up. I'm going to run to the back and see if Will is there. I'll be right back."

Moments later, Matt returned. "He's not there. I don't know what is going on."

Lauren crossed her arms as she watched more customers walk into the store. "Do you know for sure he showed up for his shift today?"

Matt nodded. "He did. I opened the store for him and gave him a briefing of everything he had to do today."

* * *

Thirty minutes later, Will was still nowhere to be found, and Lauren and Matt were handling the store's duties. Matt rang up customers and cleaned while Lauren took care of the dressing rooms and straightened up the clothing section.

Then, in walked Will, holding a huge pizza box and reeking of smoke.

Matt's eyes almost popped out of his head. "Dude. Where have you been?"

Will was taken aback. "Man, I went for my lunch break."

Matt was in shock. "You left the store without anyone working in it. We discussed that you would close the shop with a note on the door for when you took your break. Remember?"

Will paused in thought. "Oh. That's right. Completely forgot about that. Well, hopefully, nobody walked out with anything ... Or did they?"

Matt shrugged. "Only way to know is if I check the cameras, but this kind of stuff can't happen."

Will set his pizza box on the counter, took out a slice, and bit into it, oil dripping off of it onto the floor. "Whatever man. I've got to eat. So what if I forgot to lock up? Nobody shops in here anyway."

Lauren's eyes widened in disbelief at how disrespectful Will was being.

Matt picked up the pizza box and shoved it at Will. "You're fired. Go enjoy your pizza elsewhere."

Will squinted. "Fine, Man. I'll just get a job at that empanada place. That way I can get free lunch while I'm on the clock."

Matt rolled his eyes. "The empanada place closed for the season. Good luck with that."

Will strolled out of the store, not in any rush, and Matt watched as he walked down the boardwalk and out of sight. "I can't believe I hired that guy."

"Why *did* you hire him?" Lauren asked with a slight chuckle.

"Honestly, he didn't act anything like this when I met him for the interview. I feel like I've been bamboozled," Matt said.

"I'm so sorry. Hopefully, the next employee is much better," Lauren said as she stood next to Matt, staring down the boardwalk, noticing Steven in his yellow shirt stepping out of a store in the distance.

* * *

"Thank you for hosting dinner again, Matt," Lauren said as Veronica and Dan joined them in Matt's backyard oasis. It boasted plenty of places to sit, string lights, and the beautiful bay.

"It's no problem. I enjoy hosting," he said with a smile.

Dan laughed. "Good, because Lauren's house is torn up right now from all the work being done."

Matt scratched his chin. "Dan, what you're doing over there is incredible. Refinishing hardwood floors in an entire house is quite the feat."

Dan shrugged. "It is, but having help from you and Lauren's dad has made the process a lot easier. Going to start on the kitchen tomorrow, which should go a lot quicker. Laying tile is probably what I'm best at."

Veronica chuckled. "Then we have some projects back home in Vermont to take care of."

Lauren nodded and took a sip of her drink. "Matt, I can't believe you replicated the limeade from Starfish Cove. It tastes exactly the same."

Matt smiled. "Well, I'll admit I asked Travis for the recipe after seeing how much you liked it."

Lauren blushed. "You did? That was sweet of you."

Dan took a sip of his limeade. "This is good. We just had a really good drink for brunch this morning at Breezy Shores Inn. What was it again, Veronica?"

Veronica rolled her eyes. "It was some kind of pineapple-and-apple-juice concoction with sparkling water."

"You didn't like it?" Lauren asked.

Veronica shrugged. "It was alright. We just saw some upsetting things this morning that left a bad taste in my mouth."

Dan nodded. "Yeah, I forgot to mention that part."

"What happened?" Matt asked.

Veronica took a deep breath. "Well, our server accidentally mixed up our order. It wasn't a big deal, as they had it out pretty quickly afterwards, but we could see into the kitchen from where we were sitting, and the owner was screaming at our server, calling her names, and smacked the tray out of her hand. The server was in tears. It was disturbing to witness. It's been on my mind ever since."

Lauren's eyes widened as she stared over at Matt, who was looking back at her. "So, it was Charlotte, the owner? You're sure?"

"Yes. We've spoken to her a few times, so we know who she is," Dan said.

"And since she's the owner, who do we complain to? Do we complain to her about her own actions? What's she going to do? Fire herself?" Veronica asked.

Before Lauren could answer, Erin and John arrived and were walking through the backyard.

"Hey, guys!" Matt yelled out. "We've got two seats for you right here. What would you like to drink?"

"I'll take whatever beer you've got, and the missus will probably want a glass of white," John said.

Erin nodded at Matt. "If you have it. Also, we brought chips and taco dip for a little appetizer before dinner," she said, pointing at the covered glass dish in her hand.

"Perfect. Put that on the center table there, and I'll bring out some paper plates, napkins, and spoons," Matt said as he hurried inside.

After saying their hellos, Matt was back outside and handing drinks to Erin and John.

"Perfect. Thank you, Matt," Erin said as she sat in her chair. "Now, what were you all discussing before we arrived? Didn't mean to interrupt."

Dan cleared his throat. "We were discussing Breezy Shores Inn, where we're currently staying."

Veronica chimed in. "Specifically, the owner, Charlotte."

Erin took a sip of her wine and sat forward. "Before you go any further, I have something to say about that place."

John put his hand on Erin's arm. "Hon …"

Erin shook her head. "John, I need to tell them. I wanted to say this at Dock's when we were all there for dinner, but didn't feel the timing was appropriate."

Lauren scooped some taco dip on a chip and popped it into her mouth, then leaned closer to hear Erin better.

"The Breezy Shores Inn is terrible. We recommended that place to friends who came into town once. Initially, our friends were impressed. They loved the fancy outdoor areas and the remodeled room, but one night they woke up to the owner drunk in the pool with friends at 3 a.m., being loud and obnoxious. They ended up turning on a white noise app so they could drown out the noise and get some sleep."

Veronica shook her head. "We just got done telling Matt and Lauren about a disturbing incident where the owner was berating a worker to tears."

Erin nodded. "I'm not shocked by that at all. My friends

said the next day after that drunken pool escapade, they went down to brunch to find Charlotte stumbling around the lobby, looking disheveled. She was being extra nice to guests, but as soon as an employee was near, her whole demeanor changed. Just nasty and unkind. But it doesn't end there ..."

Dan glanced at Veronica. "Let's see if we can cancel our remaining nights there. I'm getting angrier by the minute about this woman taking our money."

"Fine with me," Veronica said.

"What else happened?" Matt asked Erin.

Erin cleared her throat. "That next evening, they were awoken again in the middle of the night, but not by the owner's loud noises in the pool. Oh, it was much worse. Thousands of mosquitos and gnats were swarming them in their bed. They thought they'd left the balcony door open, but it wasn't that. Turns out, there was a small gap between the balcony door and the wall. They plugged it up with a towel but had to wait until the morning to speak to someone. The owner refused to switch their room. They ended up leaving early and staying at our house the remainder of their visit. I felt absolutely terrible for recommending that place. Never again."

Lauren looked at Matt. "Well, I guess I've made my decision. Erin, you're the third person to tell me awful stories about Charlotte at the Breezy Shores Inn. The owner offered me a job during the offseason in case I keep Chipper's closed, but I'm not taking it. There's no way."

"Unless you want to get treated horribly, I recommend you don't. After we leave here, we're going to pack our things, and I'm going to attempt to get our money back for the remainder of the days we have booked there," Dan said as he dipped a chip into the taco dip. "Then, I'm writing a scathing review online. People need to be warned about that lady and the way she treats people."

Matt nodded at Lauren. "Definitely don't work there. Travis is a good man and always kind to other businesses in the area. If he doesn't like her, that's saying a lot. I'm sure something else will come up."

Lauren took a sip of her limeade. "Definitely. I'm just glad I'm hearing this now and not after I agreed to work there. By the way, what's for dinner?"

Matt looked back towards the house. "My homemade lasagna. I made a couple of pans of it. They're cooking in the oven now. There are also garlic rolls and salad. We can eat out here or inside, you guys decide."

CHAPTER TEN

"How did you get these amazing seats?" Lauren asked as she and Matt bit into their P-shaped soft pretzels.

Matt smiled as the crowd roared when the biggest homerun hitter on the Phillies came up to bat right in front of them. "A buddy of mine. He gets them through his job, and he doesn't like baseball. I always take them off his hands. Gosh, it makes me miss playing ball so much."

Lauren watched as an exciting double play was hit, and everyone around them got up out of their seats, clapping and celebrating. Lauren and Matt stood up and high-fived.

Just then, Veronica sat next to Lauren with Dan beside her. "CP Rankin Club, eh? Seems like the best seats in the house. Everything feels so close," she said as she took a bite of her burger.

"Where'd you guys end up going?" Matt asked.

"Shake Shack," Dan said as he ate some of his cheese fries.

Another Phillies player hit a pop-up that was caught, and the inning was over without any runs.

Lauren turned to Matt. "So, after yesterday, what are your plans for a new hire?"

Matt sighed. "I'm thinking about closing up the shop. I

make enough in the summer to get by for the rest of the year if I don't overspend. It's just too hard to find good help this time of the year. The college and high school students all went back to school, and a lot of the seasonal help comes in from other countries, so they also leave. Nobody else wants to work a few days a week at a surf shop in the fall from what I've found."

"You're ready to throw in the towel so soon?" Lauren asked, feeling slight concern about the situation.

Matt nodded. "Sales have dwindled every day since Labor Day. If I stay open into October, they'll probably be nonexistent by then. It just doesn't make sense financially to keep Jungle Surf open in the offseason, it seems."

Just then, a player on the opposing team hit a foul ball right at them. Lauren and Veronica ducked instinctually even though a huge net was in front of them to block the ball.

Dan and Matt laughed hard.

Veronica sat up straight in her seat. "I'm used to being way back past the nets, where you can actually catch foul balls. That's my excuse."

Lauren chuckled and looked back over at Matt. "Back to Jungle Surf, what do you usually do in the offseason when you close up shop?"

"A little of this and that," he said. "Mainly, though, I take a break, then I start planning for the year ahead by January. I figure out what sold the most and order more stock for the store, start hiring or rehiring, taking care of taxes, you know, all of that. But really, I've been toying with the idea of finding an offseason job," Matt said as he watched a couple sit down in front of them.

"What kind of job would interest you?" Lauren asked.

Matt shrugged. "Not really sure, but something not too stressful. I have enough of that running my own business," he said with a slight smile.

The inning ended without any runs, and Lauren turned to

Veronica and Dan. "So, what happened? Did you end up getting a refund from Breezy Shores Inn?"

Dan took a sip of his beer. "Actually, yeah, but it wasn't easy."

"She recognized us," Veronica said. "She remembered we were friends of yours."

"She did? How did that even come up?" Lauren asked.

Veronica glanced at the ball field and back at Lauren. "Well, we were in the lobby, basically telling her we had an emergency and couldn't stay the final days there—"

Lauren cocked her head to the side. "That was your excuse? An emergency?"

Dan nodded. "Yes. I didn't want to get into her unprofessionalism. I wasn't looking for any confrontation this morning. So, we made up a lie."

Veronica cut in. "So, Dan tells her we have an emergency, and you could tell she wasn't buying it. She was asking us all kinds of questions about the emergency, things that are, honestly, none of her business."

Dan shrugged. "Guess I'm bad at lying."

Veronica laughed. "Terrible! The owner said, 'I hope everything is OK,' and Dan says, 'It will be once we remove the raccoon.'"

Dan laughed. "It was the first thing I could think of!"

Matt chuckled. "So, it was *that* easy? You got your refund for the remaining days and checked out?"

"Not so quick," Veronica said. "She then looks us up and down and says, 'Aren't you friends of Lauren, the woman I spoke with?'"

"Oh no," Lauren said as her stomach flipped into a knot.

"It gets better," Veronica said. "We told her we were *close* friends of yours ... and she started asking all kinds of questions about you."

Matt's eyes widened. "What kind of questions?"

Dan thought for a moment. "Whether she was reliable, a

good team player, friendly ... you know, interview-type questions."

Lauren squinted. "Those are questions she should ask me, not my friends who are guests at her inn. If she wanted references—"

Veronica nodded. "Oh, we know. We also know that you didn't want the job. So, it started feeling very awkward very quickly."

Dan rubbed his hands together. "So, we get our money, throw our luggage into the car, and get out of there. It felt like a freedom drive. Veronica is driving, and I'm immediately leaving a review online."

Veronica chuckles. "He leaves this long review. All about her in the pool at 3 a.m., her berating her workers, everything we saw ...."

Dan shook his head. "And stupid me forgets that my full name will be posted, and she responds to the review within minutes."

"She must have notifications set up for reviews," Veronica said as she sipped her drink.

"Anyway, she basically caught us in our lie, as the review basically stated why we left so early ... and raccoons weren't part of the reason," Dan said as he started laughing.

"And I'm glad you don't want to work there, because I'm pretty sure we just ruined that for you," Veronica said as she bit her lip. "You still don't ... right?"

Lauren shook her head. "Absolutely not. That has already been decided on. Even if she treated me well, I'm not working for someone who treats others like that. Don't even worry."

"Phew. OK, good," Veronica said, holding her chest with relief.

Dan looked towards Matt. "Lauren, you mind switching seats with me for an inning? I want to talk to Matt."

"No problem," Lauren said as she got up and moved seats.

Veronica put her head on Lauren's shoulder. "I love baseball games. They're so nostalgic, and who doesn't love being out in the sunshine?"

Lauren nodded. "Me too. I've always loved baseball, probably because of my dad. By the way, I saw Steven yesterday."

Veronica lifted her head and stared at Lauren. "Are you serious?"

"Yes. On the boardwalk again. I was with Matt, looking at the Corvettes that were parked there for the car show. I look up, and there he is."

"Did he see you?" Veronica asked.

Lauren shook her head. "I don't think so. I made sure he didn't. I ducked behind a car, then dragged Matt into a nearby store. Matt had no clue what was going on until I finally told him."

"Why is he still here? It just boggles my mind," Veronica said as she stared out towards the field in thought.

* * *

After the game and dinner in the city, they all headed back to Bay Road in Ocean City, with Lauren driving everyone in her car.

Veronica stared at Lauren's front porch as they arrived. "It looks like there's someone sitting on your porch."

Lauren pulled the car into the driveway and stared, noticing someone was, indeed, sitting in a chair on her porch. "This a little frightening."

"I'll take care of it," Matt said as he reached for the handle.

"Me too," Dan said.

Lauren put her hand on Matt's shoulder. "Wait," she said staring. "It's Steven."

Dan sighed. "I can still handle that," he said, opening the car door.

"What do you want us to do? How about we go with you to the front door?" Veronica asked.

Lauren gulped hard. "Let me talk to him first. If you want, wait in Matt's house. He obviously wants to talk about something."

"We can do that, if that's what you want, but should we be worried about this guy? Has he ever been aggressive?" Matt asked, concerned.

Lauren shook her head. "No, just a cheater."

Veronica pursed her lips. "Yep, has that good ol' cheater title on his resume."

Matt glanced at his house. "Well, let's head over, guys. We will give them a minute."

"But we'll be within earshot. Just holler if you need us," Dan said as they all got out of the car and headed towards Matt's place.

Lauren took a deep breath, got out of the car, and walked up the front steps, looking over at Steven, who looked absolutely awful. He was barely recognizable with the bags under his eyes, dirty clothes, and messy hair.

"Hi, Steven," Lauren said delicately.

Steven sighed and looked off into the distance. "Hi."

Lauren took a seat next to him. "What's going on? I thought you went home."

Steven still stared into the distance. "I've been waiting for my car to get repaired. It broke down the first day I got here."

Lauren shifted her eyes, remembering she saw his car when she and Veronica were at Chipper's. "Your Outback?"

Steven nodded. "Yes. It's why I had the rental. They're getting the part in tomorrow, so they say."

"Well, that's good. You can get on the road back to Vermont shortly," Lauren said, trying to lighten the mood.

Steven turned his head to look at Matt's house, then looked back at Lauren. "I saw you with that guy on the boardwalk."

Lauren shrugged. "Yeah, and?"

"You're seeing someone?" Steven asked, his eyes looking glassy.

"Yes," Lauren said matter-of-factly, "I am."

Steven stared down at his hands, clearly not liking her answer.

"What are you doing here, Steven?" Lauren asked.

Steven thought for a moment. "I came to restore us to what we used to be. To apologize from the depths of my soul. I came back for you … the love of my life."

Lauren inhaled deeply and looked at the ceiling, feeling tears welling up in her eyes. "Steven, it's too late. You betrayed my trust. We've already gotten divorced, and we sold our house. It's over. It's done."

Steven gulped. "I made the biggest mistake of my life. I've ruined my life."

Lauren felt bad for him, but at the same time, she remembered all the hurt and pain he caused her, and she started to not feel so bad. "Well, you didn't have to cheat … with, what, two women? I mean, what did you expect to happen? I was going to find out one way or another. Did you think I'd stick by your side?"

"Well, you basically forced me to cheat," Steven said, growing irritated.

"I forced you? How so?" Lauren asked, her attitude coming out.

"By not providing for my needs for months," Steven said.

Lauren scratched her chin. "Oh, right … the months after I had my *surgery*. Gee, sorry I was in too much pain to walk, let alone worry about your *needs*."

Steven rolled his eyes. "Whatever. I cheated on you for years. It took you forever to find out. I'm amazed it went on so long."

Lauren was taken aback. "Years, you say?"

A switch flipped on Steven, and suddenly he went from a sad, regretful ex-husband to a heartless, arrogant one. "Yes, years. Many years. I was never playing poker with my buddies on Wednesday nights. I'll say that."

Lauren quickly racked her brain, remembering the many years he'd left to play poker. Suddenly, she felt lightheaded. "I ... I need to go," she said, quickly getting up and heading over to Matt's house. She walked up his porch steps, and Matt opened the front door, where Lauren fell into his arms with tears in her eyes.

"Are you OK?" Matt asked as he held Lauren's face and looked into her eyes.

Lauren took a deep breath then let some tears roll down her face. "He basically just admitted to me that our entire marriage was a sham. He cheated for years. Years! I didn't need to know that."

Matt shook his head in disgust and hugged Lauren tightly. "I'm so sorry this is happening. Why is he even over there?"

Lauren wiped a tear from her eye. "He wanted to get back together. He expressed his regret for everything, but when he realized I wasn't taking the bait, he got nasty."

Matt glanced at Lauren's porch—where Steven still sat, staring back at them—with daggers in his eyes. "I'm telling him to leave."

Dan came out the front door with Veronica after overhearing part of the conversation. "You need backup, Matt?"

Matt nodded. "Let's go. We'll call the cops if we need to."

Lauren and Veronica stood on the porch watching as Matt and Dan approached Steven.

Matt crossed his arms as he stood in front of Steven. "You thought you'd get back with your ex-wife by driving all the way down to her new house in a different state and *then* admitting to her you cheated for a lot longer than she'd known about? Tell me how that makes sense."

Steven rolled his eyes. "You must be the new boyfriend. What? Do you boogie board for a living?" he asked, eyeing the surfboards in the back of Matt's Jeep.

Dan chimed in. "He runs a business. Not that it's any of your concern. How about you finally leave Ocean City and get on the road. Don't come back here again."

Steven squinted. "What are you going to do about it, *Dan*?"

Dan laughed. "Well, I'll leave what I'm going to do to your imagination, but in the meantime, we're going to call the cops to get you escorted out of here."

Matt pulled out his phone, put it on speaker and started dialing.

"Fine! Fine. I'll leave," Steven said as he stumbled down the front steps towards his car parked on the other side of the street.

"My man, are you drunk?" Matt yelled out after him.

Steven didn't answer and kept walking.

"He can't drive like this," Matt said to Dan.

Dan rolled his eyes. "Fine. I'll drive his car to wherever he's staying, and you follow us."

Dan stood in front of the driver's side door as Steven tried to open it.

"Move, please," Steven said.

Dan shook his head. "You can't drive like this. If you try to, I'm definitely calling the cops, and you'll probably get a DUI. Let me know where you're staying, and I'll drive you."

Steven sighed. "Fine. The Breezy Shores Inn," he said while walking around to the passenger side and getting in.

Dan jumped in and started the car while Steven glanced over him. "Have you been to this inn? Lovely place and owner."

Dan put the car in drive and rolled his eyes.

CHAPTER ELEVEN

The next morning, Lauren arrived alone at Chipper's with her coffee. The sunlight was casting beams of light in different corners of the restaurant, and it was eerily quiet, except for the sound of tiny drops of water from a leaky kitchen faucet that hadn't been fixed yet.

She sat alone in a booth and looked around the adorably vintage restaurant, remembering all the memories she'd had there with family and friends growing up.

She looked towards the swinging door to the kitchen, thinking back to when her grandmother put her in a kid's apron with a chef's hat and had her carry out a pan full of muffins. The whole restaurant clapped, making her turn red immediately. Then during her adolescent years, she had a crush on a boy she'd met on the beach, and he showed up at Chipper's one day while Lauren was eating breakfast in a booth with friends. He sat in the booth directly behind them, and Lauren's friends giggled so loudly that Lauren had slunk down into her seat until she was almost completely under the table out of pure embarrassment.

Her thoughts were interrupted by a knock at the door. There stood George, a longtime employee of Chipper's. He was a cook but had worked his way up to manager as well. He enjoyed cooking so much that he asked to keep both positions after he was promoted.

Lauren unlocked the door and let George in. "Hey, George. What brings you here?"

George, who also had a to-go coffee, sat in the booth where Lauren had been sitting. Lauren joined him. "I heard through the grapevine that you're thinking about keeping Chipper's open during the offseason."

Lauren nodded. "I am. I'm hoping to make my decision by tomorrow."

George took a sip of his coffee. "Well, can I give you my input?"

"Definitely," Lauren said, resting her chin on her hands.

"As you know, I've worked here since your grandparents owned the place. Every year, we closed after Labor Day and reopened the weekend before Memorial Day ... except one year, we did stay open in the offseason," George said.

"Really? So my grandparents gave it a shot? I didn't know that."

George nodded. "They did indeed, and ... it failed. They barely made a profit those months. In fact, I think they lost money."

Lauren nodded. "So you're thinking it's best I stick to keeping it open seasonally?"

"Yes, but it's not because of your grandparents' lack of success that one year. Surely, you might have better success in this day and age, but really, the cooks all head back home to be with their families in the winter. The older servers that have been here forever enjoy having the fall and winter off, and the younger servers, they're back to college."

"Sounds familiar. Matt ... my ... neighbor, he's going through the same issue with his retail store," Lauren said as she sat in thought over how she should introduce Matt to people. Were they officially boyfriend and girlfriend?

George took another drink of his coffee and set the cup down on the table, which snapped Lauren out of her thoughts. "Trust me, these months go by fast. Memorial Day creeps up pretty fast, especially the older you get," he said while grabbing his coffee cup, getting up from the table, and heading towards the door. "If you want to discuss more, just give me a call. Talk soon," he said. The door slammed behind him, and the restaurant was quiet once more.

Lauren once again sat alone with her thoughts. Before she knew it, ten minutes had gone by, and she noticed a familiar face walking up the sidewalk towards the restaurant. She got up and opened the door.

"What are you up to?" Lauren playfully asked.

Matt smiled. "I don't know. I kind of wanted to see what it's like when it's empty," he said with a chuckle as he stepped inside.

"George, one of our longtime employees, just left not too long ago. He basically convinced me it's better to only stay open seasonally," Lauren said as she sat on a red stool by the counter.

Matt sat next to her. "Well, he probably knows what he's talking about."

Lauren paused in thought, then looked at Matt. "You know, I brought up your business to George, and when I mentioned who you were, I fumbled on my words. I said you were a neighbor because I wasn't sure what we are. Are we in an official relationship?"

Matt blushed. "I hope so. I've been calling you my girlfriend to others."

Lauren laughed. "You have? My gosh, I wish I'd known that. It would have made this a lot easier for me."

Matt chuckled. "I'm sorry. Should have told you I made you my girlfriend."

Lauren grew quiet. "Look, I want to thank you for yesterday ... with Steven."

Matt nodded. "It's fine. I've been the designated driver for many drunk friends over the years."

"Not just that. Thank you for still being here after all that drama with my ex-husband. My gosh, that would be enough to scare anyone away," Lauren said as she lightly touched Matt's hand.

Matt sighed and looked up at the ceiling. "I guess now is a good time to bring up my experience with *this*."

"*Your* experience?" Lauren asked.

Matt nodded. "Unfortunately, I've had somewhat of a similar situation. It wasn't with my ex-wife, though. After we divorced, I dated for a few years. A lot of them were nice women, but it just didn't work out one way or the other, but there was one …"

Lauren's eyes widened. "Oh no. Was it bad?"

Matt took a deep breath. "Bad is an understatement. I don't bring this up to anyone. My family doesn't even know about it. I had started dating a woman that I met on a dating app. She lived in Philly, which is a bit of a drive, but we decided to see what came of it anyway. We had a couple great dates in Philadelphia and a couple here in Ocean City. Everything felt like it was going wonderfully. Then, one evening after work, I get home to find the lights on in my house, which was odd. I open the door and find Talia sitting on my couch, uninvited."

"Did she have a key?" Lauren asked, surprised.

Matt shook his head. "No, and I hadn't given her one or told her where I hid the spare key. She just looked for it and happened to find it. I kept it under a potted fern."

Lauren shifted her eyes. "You have like five potted ferns on the porch."

Matt nodded. "Right, and back then, there were more."

"So, she probably looked under each pot …" Lauren said, trailing off into thought. "This is actually quite frightening."

Matt sighed. "Yes, it was."

A shiver went down Lauren's spine. "I guess Steven sitting on my porch pales in comparison. What happened after you went inside?" Lauren asked.

Matt thought for a moment. "Well, this is where it gets really scary. Turns out, she was an extremely jealous person, and she was very insecure about my ex-wife. She snooped around my house, pulled out old photo albums, and tried to log into my laptop and other devices, unsuccessfully."

"What?!" Lauren yelled out.

"Thankfully, those things are password protected, but she probably would have snooped in my emails and everything," Matt said.

"How did you get her to leave?"

"I called the cops. She wouldn't leave when I asked. Instead, she sobbed and screamed at me, as though we had been dating for five years and she'd just found out something terrible about me. It was absolutely unreal," Matt said.

"So, the cops came?" Lauren asked, still finding such a story hard to believe.

"They showed up alright, and they had to physically get her out of the house. She put up a fight. After that, I never hid a key outside again. I also changed my locks just to be safe. So, if you're worried that I was scared off about your ex sitting on your porch, been there done that," he said with a laugh.

* * *

"This is really cool that Travis and Kelly invited us," Lauren said as she, Matt, Veronica, and Dan walked through Ocean City on their way to Starfish Cove Inn.

"I'm excited. They do this stargazing event once or twice a year, and I always miss it. They bring in a local astronomer. It's pretty neat," Matt said as he put his arm around Lauren.

"You guys good back there?" Lauren asked as she looked

behind her to see Dan and Veronica holding hands, happily strolling along.

"Never been better," Dan said with a smile.

They got to Starfish Cove, walked in, and were greeted by Travis in the kitchen. "Hey, guys, you're early. Justin, our astronomer, should be here in a half hour. We've got seats set up out back and snacks and drinks inside. Help yourself while you wait," he said as he chopped carrot sticks on a cutting board with a dish towel flung over his shoulder.

"Matt!" a voice yelled from the stairs. "Where have you been all of my life?!"

Matt laughed as he saw Kelly coming down the stairs, her long flowy skirt dragging on the ground behind her. "Great to see you, Kel," Matt said as they gave each other a hug. "This is my girlfriend, Lauren, and these are her friends Veronica and Dan," he said pointing.

"Wonderful to meet you all," she said, whipping her long braid behind her shoulder. "Just absolutely amazing really."

"It's a beautiful place you have here," Lauren said, smiling.

Kelly sighed and glanced around the room, feeling proud. "Thank you. We put a lot of hard work into this inn to make it what it is. It's our baby. Would you like the grand tour?" she asked enthusiastically.

"Absolutely," Veronica said as she glanced at Lauren and Dan.

Matt chuckled. "I've already seen all its splendor. I'll hang here and catch up with Travis."

"OK, let's start with the upstairs and work our way down," Kelly said as she motioned for them to follow her. She got to the first room. "Now, I obviously can't show you every room, as we do have guests staying here, but I will show you the empty ones. Each room is unique," she said while opening the door.

Lauren's mouth dropped open. "Wow. This is absolutely stunning, Kelly," she said as they walked in and marveled at the four-post canopy bed.

"We use the finest bedding for sheets, pillows, and comforters. It's a must for a good night's sleep," she said while turning around. "Then, there's the gas fireplace for our offseason guests that want a little more warmth."

Dan knocked on the wall. "Plaster?"

Kelly nodded. "Yes, the original walls are still in place," she said as she peeked out the window. "Now, this room has great views of the sunset. So, we call it our Sunset Room."

"Do you have a Sunrise Room on the other side of the house?" Veronica asked.

"Yes!" Kelly said, smiling. "You're catching on," she said while walking towards the bathroom. "Now, each room comes with its own private bathroom."

Dan peeked in. "Looks great. Tiling looks new."

"The tiling is about five years old. The bathrooms definitely didn't hold up as well as the rest of the house over the years. So, we put in new showers, tubs, sinks, all of that. We want our guests to feel they're in a clean, comfortable space," Kelly said as she shut the bathroom door.

Just then, Travis yelled from downstairs. "Kelly, you up there?! We have some friends here."

"Excuse me," Kelly said as she headed back down the stairs.

Veronica sat on the bed. "I would have been happier staying here instead of Breezy Shores Inn. It feels so much cozier and homier. It's soothing."

Dan nodded. "It's got that vintage charm. There's always something special about that."

Lauren looked around the room, then towards the stairs. "I don't think she's coming back. Want to head back downstairs and get some snacks and drinks?"

"I thought you'd never ask. I'm starving," Dan said as he and Veronica followed Lauren down the steps.

Kelly was down there talking to a group of individuals while Travis and Matt were both cutting celery together. Matt looked up, noticing Lauren, Veronica, and Dan. "Did you get the tour?"

"We got an abbreviated tour, but this buffalo chicken dip looks really good," Lauren said as she grabbed a plate.

Kelly stopped talking to the group and came over to Lauren, Dan, and Veronica. "Sorry, guys. We had a bunch of inn owners from around town show up. They're also joining us for the stargazing event."

Lauren smiled. "That's so cool that you all support each other's events."

Kelly nodded. "Oh, yes. We're all friends. It's like a community of people that help each other out. We share recipes and cleaning tips. We fill in for each other if someone is sick. We even pass around names of bad customers," she said under her breath. "It's wonderful."

"I love that. You know, Travis was telling us about Breezy Shores Inn …"

Before Lauren could finish, Kelly shook her head. "Let's not even bring up her name."

"Whose name?" Randy, the owner of Turtle Island Inn, asked.

Kelly rolled her eyes. "You know who."

"Charlotte?" Randy asked.

"Well, I was trying not say it, but yes, her," Kelly said.

"Did you hear what happened?" Randy asked.

Kelly shook her head. "What now?"

"Her brother is trying to get the inn back. Apparently, Charlotte took it over without any legal right to do so. So, get out the popcorn, and let's hope this has a happy ending … for all of us in Ocean City."

"Well, golly. I never thought I'd see the day," Kelly said as she adjusted the bowl of chips. "She gives us inn owners a bad name. I hope her brother wins and wins good. He can call me if he needs a testimony."

Just then, a man with round wire-rim glasses and a telescope walked through the door. "Hi, everyone! You ready to see those stars tonight?"

"Justin! My man!" Travis yelled over the loud room. "Thank you for coming. We're really looking forward to this tonight. We've got a full group of people too."

Justin nodded. "Perfect. We should be able to get a good look at some planets and constellations tonight. It's going to be a good one."

Lauren grew excited not just to see the stars, but to be around such a cool group of people that all seemed to get along. She glanced at Matt, who was busy talking to Veronica and Dan. He had befriended her friends so easily and made them feel at home. It was more than she could ask for in a boyfriend. She felt at peace.

CHAPTER TWELVE

Early in the morning, Lauren walked to her front door and stepped out onto the porch with her hot coffee mug while Veronica and Dan slept in.

The house was officially done. She turned around and walked back inside, stopping in the foyer to take it all in. The hardwood floors were sanded, stained and sealed, and absolutely stunning. She walked into the living room—the room she was most proud of. Not only had the old carpet been ripped up, but the wicker furniture that came with the house was gone, and her comfortable and stylish furniture took its place. The walls were now white, and the beautiful trim that had been previously painted over was now back to being the original wood color. The pink lace curtains and white shades had been replaced with bamboo shades.

She walked into the dining room, where the newly tuned piano sat adorned with the gold lamp Veronica had bought her. In the middle of the room was Lauren's dining room table with a new light fixture above. The walls were painted white, just like the rest of the house.

Then, there was the kitchen. The cabinets were now hunter green, and new gold hardware pulls had been added, which changed the look drastically. White subway tiles were put in as a backsplash, and distressed wood-like tiles were on the ground. Her newly acquired stained-glass floral piece hung in front of the window over the kitchen sink. It was like a kitchen from a magazine.

She heard steps coming down the stairs, then, "Morning," Veronica said as she yawned.

"Morning." Lauren smiled. "I bought bagels if you want one. Cream cheese too."

"That would be great. We would love that," Veronica said, still half asleep. "I have to get Dan up. We need to get back on the road soon," she said, staring around the room. "Gosh, it's beautiful in here, isn't it?"

Lauren nodded. "It's absolutely amazing. I finally feel like this is *my* home. I can't thank you and Dan enough."

"You've thanked us plenty. Trust me," Veronica said with a chuckle as she cut a cheddar bagel and put it into the toaster.

A knock came at the door, and Lauren noticed it was Matt, so she waved him in.

"Morning, everyone," Matt said, as he ran his hand through his damp, salty hair. "Just rode some amazing waves. It was bliss. Got up nice and early," he said, glancing around the kitchen. "By the way, wow. This house is totally transformed."

"Right?!" Lauren said back, enthusiastically.

Veronica quickly smeared cream cheese on the bagel and walked towards the stairs. "I don't want anyone seeing me looking like this. Sorry, Matt," she said, heading upstairs.

Lauren shrugged and laughed. "She's funny. She looks fine."

Matt crossed his arms and leaned on the counter. "Did you make your mind up about Chipper's?"

"Yes, it's staying closed. It's easier that way. What about Jungle Surf? Did you make your final decision?" Lauren asked.

Matt nodded. "Closing it up today."

"Well, now comes the part of what will we do next," Lauren said as she playfully nudged Matt.

"What do you want to do next?" Matt asked.

Lauren thought for a moment. "Go boating through the back bay near the wetlands."

"Really? That's next on your agenda?"

"Yes, I was hoping you'd come," Lauren said with a smile. "Veronica and Dan leave in about an hour for Vermont. The rest of my day is free."

Matt thought for a moment. "OK. I have some contacts. I can probably get us a little four-seater boat for the day, but first come with me to Jungle Surf to close up for the season. I'm eager to be done. With the two of us, we can be out of there by noon and in the boat sometime after."

* * *

By 9 a.m., Veronica and Dan were on the road and Matt and Lauren were walking along the boardwalk towards Jungle Surf.

Matt looked around, only noticing one person jogging up ahead of them. "Where did the crowd go?"

Lauren looked up ahead, seeing a few scattered groups of people. "Maybe they'll be here for a lunchtime walk?"

Matt nodded. "As a local who lives here, I love having the boardwalk to myself. As a business owner, I like it crowded. I'm always torn," he said with a chuckle.

They got to Jungle Surf, and Matt unlocked the door and stepped inside with Lauren behind him. "What are you going to do with all the plants?"

"They're coming home with me. They won't get enough sunlight with the doors shut. I'll make space on my sun porch for them. I have some boxes and a dolly we can wheel them out on," Matt said as he walked towards the back.

"And the clothes?" Lauren yelled back towards him.

"That all stays. The books, the sunblock, surfboards. All of it can stay. I'm going to cover it all up with plastic to keep dust off it, though," he said as he approached with three large boxes.

Lauren put a few succulents, cacti, and bird's nest ferns into a box, then she looked up and noticed a wooden tuxedo cat figure wearing a chain necklace next to the monstera plant.

"I love this," Lauren said as she picked up the wooden cat.

Matt smiled. "Me too. Reminds me of my ol' boy Roscoe. Best cat I ever had."

"I didn't know you were a cat person," Lauren said, smiling.

Matt nodded. "Big cat guy. I even helped trap and neuter a colony of feral cats a year or so ago. It was a huge undertaking, but we got it done with the help of a local rescue. But Roscoe ... he was my pride and joy. He passed last year."

"There's actually an older tuxedo cat at Mew to You over on Asbury that I have my eye on. He seems really sweet. I figured we could get our new beginning together here in Ocean City," Lauren said.

Matt stopped what he was doing. "Really? Have you met him yet?"

Lauren shook her head. "I'm not even sure it's a boy. I only saw him through the glass window, but he was so sweet with the volunteer."

Matt paused in thought. "Well, I propose we get everything covered in here, get the plants in my car, then we head over to meet the tuxedo boy. I think we can squeeze it all in. Then, we can get in our boat ride and catch the sunset."

* * *

A few hours later, Matt and Lauren were in the cat room at Mew to You. They had found out the older tuxedo cat was named Scout, and he was ten years old and a complete lap cat who had taken a liking to Matt immediately.

Lauren laughed as she watched Scout make himself comfortable in Matt's lap. "I don't know who should be adopting him. You or me?"

Matt nodded as he petted Scout, who was purring furiously. "Well, if you're not going to, I will. He reminds me of my Roscoe to a T. Roscoe would do exactly this."

Lauren's heart warmed as she watched Matt and Scout bond. "I think you should have him. It seems meant to be. Maybe I was just the messenger. Plus, I'll see him all the time."

"I don't know …" Matt said. Then, he looked down and saw Scout was staring him in the eyes and let out a little *meow*. "OK, fine."

* * *

Thirty minutes later, Matt had filled out an application for Scout, and they were in the car, heading to the marina to pick up the boat rental. Matt pulled into the parking lot, where they both got out and started walking to the slips. "The skiff may not be much, but it will get us out on the water."

"That's perfect," Lauren said as they both got into the small boat, and Matt started up the engine.

Matt drove the boat out onto the back bay, slowly passing through the calm marshes and wetlands. "See those buoys? There are crab traps underneath them. That way, crabbers can find them when they come back," Matt said, pointing.

Lauren lowered her sunglasses, noticing a couple men ahead of them were pulling up their crab trap. "Look there. I wonder if they got anything."

Matt slowed the boat, and they watched as the men opened their trap, pulling out two small crabs. They promptly threw them back into the water. "Doesn't look like they did," Matt said as he watched two kayakers paddle by them.

Lauren took a deep breath of the salty, marshy air and exhaled, then listened to the soft sound of water lapping around them. "I could be out here every day. It's so serene. I love that there're so many different animals out here. It's their home and our little paradise at the same time."

Matt looked off into the distance. "The sun is setting. Pretty soon after it sets we'll see the sunglow hitting everything around us. We've got a front-row seat to this beauty."

Lauren squeezed in next to Matt and put her arms around him. He, in turn, kissed her head. They heard shorebirds in the distance, the water softly hitting the boat, and a few other boaters and kayakers talking.

The sun turned the sky orange and pink as it set before them. Suddenly, everything felt like it made sense in life. She was meant to come to Ocean City all along. She was meant to be here in this moment with Matt.

EPILOGUE

A week later, Lauren went to visit her parents at their home. She walked in their door to the smell of a pot roast cooking and, of course, the Phillies game on television.

"How's the house coming along?" Joe, her dad, asked.

Lauren put her purse down on a chair. "Amazing. I spent the past week hanging art on the walls and getting the area rugs put down. It feels more like home than ever."

Nancy, her mom, washed her hands at the sink. "Good. Next, you can tackle that backyard. Make something of it. It's just grass and weeds."

Lauren nodded. "I know. It's kind of boring. I need to figure that out. Maybe Matt will give me some tips. His yard is incredible." Just then, Lauren's phone rang. It was Matt. "Hey," Lauren answered.

"What are you up to?" Matt asked as he petted Scout in his lap.

"Just stopped in to visit with my parents."

"Is that Matt?! Tell him to come over for some pot roast!" Nancy yelled from the kitchen.

Lauren laughed. "Want some pot roast? If so, come on over."

Matt chuckled. "I just ate, but tell them I'll take a rain check. Listen, I just talked to Travis …"

"Oh yeah? What's going on with him?" Lauren asked.

"Well, he and Kelly have been talking about taking some down time in the offseason. They want more time with their kids since they're so busy in the summer. Travis knows you and I both have seasonal businesses, and they asked if we'd be interested in helping run the inn part time."

"Seriously?" Lauren asked.

Matt nodded. "Oh, he and Kelly are definitely serious. I think Kelly really likes you. She's the one who came up with the idea after meeting you."

"What would we be doing?" Lauren asked.

Matt shrugged. "Checking people in and out. Getting the breakfast prepared and the snacks and drinks. Probably some cleaning—though they do have a cleaner come in once a week. Helping with any events they have going on."

Lauren plopped into her parents' recliner. "I mean, it sounds lovely, but is this something that would interest you?"

Matt laughed. "It's not really a job I'd go for, but when they said they wanted us together as a team, that appealed to me. I think we could run an inn together like a well-oiled machine. What do you think?"

Lauren smiled. "I think we should tell them yes."

* * *

Pick up book 3 in the Ocean City Tides Series, **Ocean City Midnights,** to follow Lauren, Matt, and the rest of the bunch.

Have you read the Cape May Series? If not, start with book 1, **The Cape May Garden**.

ABOUT THE AUTHOR

Claudia Vance is a writer of women's fiction and clean romance. She writes feel good reads that take you to places you'd like to visit with characters you'd want to get to know.

She lives with her boyfriend and two cats in a charming small town in New Jersey, not too far from the beautiful beach town of Cape May. She worked behind the scenes on television shows and film sets for many years, and she's an avid gardener and nature lover.

Copyright © 2025 by Claudia Vance

All rights reserved.

No part of this book may be reproduced in any form or by any electronic or mechanical means, including information storage and retrieval systems, without written permission from the author, except for the use of brief quotations in a book review.

* * *

This is a work of fiction. Names, places, events, organizations, characters, and businesses are used in a fictitious manner or the product of the author's imagination.

Made in the USA
Middletown, DE
04 June 2025